UNKNOWN LANGUAGE

UNKNOWN LANGUAGE

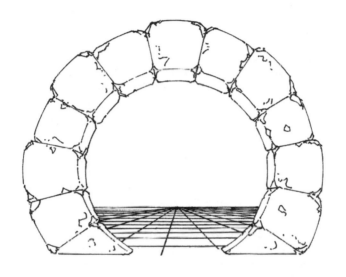

by HILDEGARD OF BINGEN
and HUW LEMMEY

with BHANU KAPIL *and* ALICE SPAWLS

First published by Ignota 2020
© Huw Lemmey and the publisher

ISBN-13: 978-1-9996759-9-8

Design by Cecilia Serafini
Endpaper image 'Vision of the angelic hierarchy'
by Hildegard of Bingen
Typeset in Palatino and Optima by Marsha Swan
Printed and bound in the UK by TJ Books Limited
Hildegard, Saint (1098–1179)

3 5 7 9 10 8 6 4 2

ignota.org

Contents

PINKY AGARWALIA
Biography of a Child Saint
in Ten Parts

BHANU KAPIL

1. The lore of the fragment was what brought us together, like wasps licking a wooden frame to build their nests. Each time we heard the story we took some of it back, in our mouths, like damp chemicals or pulp + saliva. Then spat it out to fill a hole or make the wall stronger.

I am new to writing. Is the notebook a time crystal?

Mother: 'Behind the curtain of blood I saw a shape.' That shape was an equation. Equation, constellation. What happens when we experience the Mother's love?

Father: 'I saw a terrible thing. It was after the war. A mother on the ground . . . her baby rooting for milk, suckling her . . . even though . . .'

Is the Mother a gap on the physical level that links human beings together in a sense of united loss?

Tried to get these questions out. Can't focus.

Mother: 'What would you like to feel?'

Father: 'Get me tea, and the paper.'

These are examples of communal lore. How we were when we were together and what it was like when we were apart. Also: orange grasses, foxglove, conifer, mango, dolphin, bitch.

I heard a story of a Mother and Father who loved each other so much they had an operation to remove the hearts from their bodies then sew them into each other's parts.

It must have been so chilly, like an eclipse made visible only when photographed, when the time came to lift the organs out with a powerful, single movement and give them to a nurse.

'I tell her that rocks like meteorites retain light, a sensible energy thought into substance by experiencing it,' writes the poet of another era, putting forward an idea of writing that resembles transcription, connection with a reader, but also loss.

A scrawl, a scribble.

I'm no saint.

2. I want to live a simple, beautiful life with memories and friends. I do not want to die of carotid ill health or by the hand of another.

In stating what I want and what I do not want, I practice a form of positive desire, the spirituality of a bygone era.

Imagine a February morning in 1997 or 2019, the bright green grass and the ten black ravens hopping across the lawn on the outskirts of a city filled with knaves, dolls, bears and gymnasts, but also clerics who abandoned their calling to become what we all were in the end: a ruined self.

Now gone.

Something happened.

If an ancestor is someone you can still tell a story of, then perhaps I am not a descendant.

On the planet Avaaz, where a city once was, is now a hole. Imagine a house bursting into flames in the rear-view mirror of a yellow-and-black taxi.

At the rim of this hole are low hills or mounds, forest-green and gleaming with bouncy eyes. Rat, lion, piglet, boar, cat, dog, snake, cow, sheep, rabbit, horse. Ex-zoo, this is less a wilderness than the end of cages. Here, the lion eats the horse, the snake bites the dog and the rat nips at the heel of the cow.

Can animals save us, or will it be the plants who become conscious, adept, empathetic: the functional adults of our universe?

To answer these questions, I left my home for the rim.

I was a child and perhaps I am still a child.

Lick a rose for its dew.

Wash your face when it rains.

Don't drink from the tap.

I know what to do.

3. Imagine reincarnating as a sea creature.

Imagine reincarnating in 1993, if you were born in 2023. Or 2121, if you were born in 2021.

Can we reincarnate in a society or an ocean that precedes us in the timeline of a) antiquity or b) apocalypse? Imagine the shattered turquoise or aquamarine shard of the fresco, underfoot. Imagine family time.

Turns out the apocalypse is boring and sensible, a combination of sugars, fats, and trying to come up with a cunning plan.

My suicide is more beautiful than your life, murmurs Father on the floor of the stable, where he has curled up in the place where horses once lay to take his pills.

If you are reading these words in the last century, I understand that you loved a film called *Melancholia* starring Kiefer Sutherland. If you are reading these words in the coming century, Kiefer Sutherland was a loser poet. He was not a friend to his daughter or wife. Another planet appeared in the sky, a charged form of nudity that illuminated the siblings in the film, as well as the parent–child bond.

Who is reading these words?

Who is your partner in life?

Was the person who saved our planet a devoted scientist who made room for new feelings in the space between their body and yours?

What saved us in the end? Was it food?

Meanwhile, the sun evolves every single day into something else, something further from 'sun'.

Because I was not part of a group, I knew that sexual trauma was a likelihood.

This is why I had to leave.

Like a vector, I parsed the countryside, nibbling stream mint, cowslip, lily and dill.

To survive.

4. The city is behind me now, releasing energy that is immediately channelled to anyone who needs it.

Self-induced stress and fear are the most toxic things to the system, said Mother one day, on the couch. I remember what she said because the next day her loving support was gone.

Do you know why? Ancestor, why didn't you change your ways in advance of the destruction that rendered memories into oil? Descendant, contextually, you're a miracle.

Below the flag of Avaaz and above the harbour, a body emerges from an outline of golden light: the citizen host. No, I don't know who this is.

I ran from the glowing body that was unrecognisable to me.

It was stressful. I was scared. It was toxic!

The body I saw was like an invisible painting that becomes apparent when water is dropped upon it.

I ran from this new art.

Towards the trees where something, I could hear, was making a sound.

A sound, a prefix, a tone.

'Attune yourself to inner magnetism,' said the predator.

But I fled – something the predator did not expect.

Ancestor, what did you do in such moments, when all those sweet things were in smithereens? How did you skirt the new dominance? What were your strategies and formulas? How did you remember your Mother's face in ordinary moments? Did you have access to what we know now, the idea of the body as remembering everything that ever happened? Tell me about the dandelion and the pear tree. Tell me where you are from.

Descendant, if you are child, when the world splits into three parts, flee.

To the rim.

5. I saw an amazing thing as I lay in the straw.

Last night, I dreamed that behind the waterfall was a form of writing I could not read, something like a scrawled prescription or scroll with only the letters H, I, N and E still legible.

The night decants the moonlight over the nettles along the brook. 'Solidarity not charity,' chants the leader of a temporary camp, in the paternalistic tone I've come to recognise as a weak disguise. So, I push on, slipping away from the fire, walking as far as I can beneath the full moon the colour of a ripe plum.

August + December - February = June?

The footpath throws me into time and I walk until there it is, like the skirt of a dress filled with snakes or doves, or the roar of a cafeteria.

The waterfall.

Behind the waterfall is a cave.

I step out onto the wet, broad stone without shame or anger.

Am I a moon bird?

Look how lightly I step from the bank to the ledge, my right hand clinging to the stone of the cliff and the fingertips of my left hand extending towards, then through, the water.

Then all of me is inside, not outside.

This is what I see: a small fire, recently lit and fragrant, packed tightly into a circle of heavy stones. Each stone has a red oval painted on its roundest part, ringed with gold paint, then a thinner line of turquoise pigment or dye.

There's a kerosene stove with a kettle on it, singing at the boil.

A low wooden desk with a cushion to sit on. Someone has painted the cream fabric of the cushion with lemon, emerald-green and red paisley swirls. On the desk, wrapped in gold silk, is a book. Nobody is here. In this context, I hear two words.

Open it.

6. Kneel down in the boggling mud.

So icy.

Here.

Yes, I am speaking now. As Pinky scrambles up the scree.

Imagine a flame balanced in a bowl of water or in the bubbling spring at the origin of rivers, hovering there.

Here, a third stream comes from underneath with the energy of a fountain. Is this the history of rivers? Is an origin a confluence?

Dear Pinky, in the fourteenth minute of this new galaxy and in the last few moments of your own child-hood, I am communicating with you.

Like this.

Pinky, can you hear me?

This is the place.

Put your hand in the water. Yes, that's it . . . as far as it can go.

Blood angels calve in the moonlight, but you'll never see such a thing.

There. That's it. Pull it out now.

Right out of the water and the mud and the flame and the ice and the muck and the bright.

That's it, my lovely.

Reach in.

Can you hear me?

'Yes, I can hear you.' – Pinky to Hildegard, who has begun to speak.

7. There are forests here and snowdrops in abundance. I never imagined being here. Did you?

From agar, from flock, from lovers, from bodies that flush with warmth, from the cultural memory of lighthouses, polar bears, the revolutionary nature of young people all over the earth, something was preserved. I can feel it here, for the first time, with you.

Imagine a bunch of carrots with soil still caked on them, green tops like ferns. Or imagine the sound of a wooden flute beyond the Mughal labyrinth. Imagine the national flowers of contested regions. Every person who travelled here is unsteady, I can feel that.

Dehydrated.

If home is found on both sides of the globe, home is of course here, and always a missed land, said the poet, with whom we can still feel an emotional affinity, though he is long gone. The delicate works of that earlier time will never be kept on record now. It is up to us to memorise them; poems by people who have been incarcerated, poems by people who left their homes, poems constructed with paper and string.

Things that happened, things that might happen, on the planet Avaaz.

Here is the fragment.

[Pinky Agarwalia gestures to a chunk of ice on the tall wooden table, addressing the group. The ice is luminous, almost neon, rotating to the left then back again (twitching) without any effort or contact from Pinky herself, or the members of her audience, who are seated on the floor or leaning against the sides of the cave.]

'As you can see,' continues Pinky in a formal tone, 'the fragment is a six-dimensional object that we have to integrate. It's evolving. We don't have much time.'

The ice has a lower luminosity than what it contains and so the light from the fragment crosses two frequencies, like an unknown language. Some photons can't escape the staggered mesh.

How will we melt this ice that does not melt when we heat it or crack when we smash it on the ground?

Pinky taps the book.

8. An unknown language is a rose meteor, because what doesn't ebb off leaves lines.

An unknown language is held in a quasi-steady state until someone reads it for the first time. Then it becomes toroidal, streaming lines.

An unknown language is nondimensional and so it can't be written down. So, what are you looking at?

You need a code to look at the unknown language.

Encased in ice, a word vibrates.

Discontinuous spikes pulse in the body of the viewer.

It helps to wear damp silk. The coolness calms the vagus nerve, a nerve that wraps around the heart as it travels from gut to brain.

The fragment of an unknown language is unstable, convective, buoyant, and can't be extracted, just as the real universe can't be plotted.

Is the one you love a proxy for radiance? (Hildegard, the chameleon.)

Is the fragment a cosmological simulation? (Hildegard, who ingested galantine, converting the energy of her life into an identity as bright as six billion suns.)

An unknown language comes from a foreign place, like a sample of the life once lived there.

An unknown language is a very rich source, a repository of shared information, like an amethyst cave at the place where the river meets the sea.

Herbs and bodywork relieve the build-up of tension. (Hildegard, off-message.)

Hildegard, you were so close to me at the origin of rivers and then in the cave. Was it you who were so recently there, stoking the fire with the toe of your pointed boot?

Hildegard, your metamorphosis, like an animal or fish, keeps slipping through my hands.

I follow your command.

9. Like a text that is destined to be read as a sign might, the book was a series of commands. As Pinky read each sentence in turn, the words lit up with a weak flame, one by one, so that when Pinky finished reading, there was no book.

Red flowers, a moorhen. Pinky waited until the spring came before she left the cave and returned to the camp below, where other orphans had gathered, sitting with their backs to nature out of a sadness they couldn't stop.

To whisper, follow me.

Up and up to the origin of rivers went the children, on Pinky's heel.

For her eyes were shining.

Whoever followed her stopped asking, *What is happening to me?*

Hot water sipped upon waking. A branch to chew on that cleaned the teeth and nourished the breath. Vegetables, seeds, black tea. 'Mandala for the unde-fended heart,' said Pinky, when one of the orphans asked her what she was drawing.

The cave was like a violet door in the side of the mountain.

There was a way to enter and another way to leave, to relieve the bowels in a wood, a shovel in hand to dig a hole and refill it.

I can compete with you in the body I have. This was a new thought, one of many the orphans had, individually.

Soon it was time to gather.

'It's time,' said Pinky.

Let's begin.

Once they were ready, the children or near-children or ex-children gathered in a circle within view of the cascade, which was Prussian blue and sparkling in the early morning light.

In the middle was the block of ice.

10. With the fingertip of your fourth finger touch the bone of your heart and with your other hand touch the ground.

In the years to come, we would learn from our failures and write about what we left behind. Our writing took the form of stories and poems, which we shared in the woodland clearing where we met to learn from each other. There wasn't a university in our future, and there never would be again. Instead, we apprenticed to our elders, then shared in their care.

That morning, the morning of our first ritual, we looked at each other like shy swans, bending our necks to look down, and then up again.

Pinky, now our leader, repeated the instructions in a clear voice, and we remembered the book which had set itself on fire as she read, each word in turn. Was this our mythology?

The paper's hiss. Ash on the fingertips. ABC flame.

The final instruction was this: *Bring to mind an experience of hatred.*

The gold light descended then from the crown to the heart, dissolving the head of the enemy, the regret, the pain.

Pinky set the chunk of ice at the centre of our circle, on the ground.

We visualised the gold light extending from our hearts.

To pierce the chemistry of the fragment.

Imagine twenty spokes of the brightest light you have ever seen.

As the ice shatters, a sound is released.

A new sound which reaches us as pale green light, vibrating lightly, lightly, like bees but also flowers.

Is a stamen a tuning fork? The Pleiades, above us, tilt.

In synchrony.

Was this the moment that our species took a turn?

TO BE CONTINUED!!!

Mei-mei Berssenbrugge's *A Treatise on Stars* (2020) and Agha Shahid Ali's ghazal, 'Land' (2001), are the two works of poetry I reference. The line 'I saw an amazing thing as I lay in the straw' is from a monologue I memorised as a teenager, but I have perhaps misremembered as I cannot find the source text. The phrase 'shy swans' derives from a description of ponies in James Wright's 'A Blessing': 'They bow shyly as wet swans. They love each other. / There is no loneliness like theirs.' The spacetime vocabulary comes out of talks and lectures at the Kavli Institute for Cosmology in 2019 and early 2020. The way of speaking to ancestors and descendants, across time, comes from Joanna Macy's *The Work That Reconnects*, a practice I was first introduced to by Regina Smith at Naropa University. The imagery of 'national flowers of contested regions' comes from Iftikhar Dadi and Elizabeth Dadi's *Efflorescence* series (2013–19), and their installation at Kettle's Yard, part of the exhibition *Homelands: Art from Bangladesh, India and Pakistan* (2019). The cave behind the waterfall is a cave I myself visited as a child. There, I was served tea by the person who lived inside it, perched on a hand-woven stool. The curtain of blood appearing in the mind, and through it the equation's proof, comes from a story of the mathematician, Srinivasa Ramanujan, whose vision of Mahalakshmi this was. The phrase 'unknown language' comes from Hildegard of Bingen, a twelfth-century mystic, as channelled by Pinky Agarwalia, an orphan of what was once Earth and is now Avaaz. Pinky divines then perpetuates Hildegard's instructions in 2121, the year of devastating ecological norms, species mutation, and new ideas of education, healing and love. Imagine quantum laser beams shining from the shabby little hearts of twenty orphans, in a variant of the spiritual practice Chöd. Imagine an alphabetic fragment encased in ice that does not melt in fire nor shatter when you throw it on the ground. The ice signifies, perhaps, forms of trauma that are intractable, yet which also preserve something, or protect it from destruction. Are all biographies a study of surviving something we were only passing through?

UNKNOWN LANGUAGE

But although I heard and saw these things, because of doubt and low opinion of myself and because of diverse sayings of men, I refused for a long time a call to write, not out of stubbornness but out of humility, until weighed down by a scourge of God, I fell onto a bed of sickness.

Hildegard of Bingen

PART I

I

A SCREECH PIERCED my fragile sleep, tearing my consciousness, as one half stayed with the shadow world and the other was pulled into the light. It sounded as though an eagle had struck someone from a height – rushing, accompanied by a horrible, high-pitched wail. I sat bolt upright, clutching the sheets to my body, and situated myself: the sound was a refuse truck in the street below my apartment. I wiped the sweat of the clammy night from my brow and picked up the medical journal I had discarded by my bedside six hours before, but the words wouldn't focus and the thought of the day to come filled me with nervous tension. All fear the dark nights of the soul, yet the toils of the day are no less wretched. It was not life or death that troubled me, just some simple administrative task. The chance for sleep had passed. My throat was filled with sputum made worse by the fine dust that fell from the worm-eaten rafters. I opened the balcony shutters to the barely dawning day; no better time to stroll out into the city.

I passed through the narrow alleys that cut from my neighbourhood to the rougher quarters. The paths opened into a broad, landscaped park, built upon some old citadel or palace, long since ploughed back into the earth. I sat beside the fountain that was sculpted into the shape of what we then assumed a seraph would look like, before we knew. A cherubic youth, fattened like a piglet around the wrists and legs, yet weightless on his stone wings. His cheeks were full like ripening pomegranates, and he spurted water from his mouth. A breeze caught the stream, dispersing a mist which formed a slight chlorinated sheen on my lips. The grass too was developing its morning dew, a silvery sparkle as the sun began to creep over the parapets of the city walls.

It is at dawn that the smaragdus, the emerald, is formed. This is the tranquil time when things swell with the properties they will hold for the rest of the day. Oranges expand on their trees; the lamb suckles at its mother's teat as the first rays of sun spread their warmth. Herbs absorb their potent properties from the damp air, and make it fragrant in return. The smaragdus gains all its energies in this moment, engorged by the first light – energies that bestow only positive attributes upon us. For this reason, the stone finds its restorative position inside the human mouth, that moist lock that channels light down into the darkness of the gut.

The walk had cleared my throat but on my way home, I found myself hacking up more sputum. My bronchial tract felt corrupted and rotten, like the dank alleys I tread. It seemed as though this same cough was blowing out of every waking bedroom over the street – six storeys of mediaeval filth, whores and pimps in tiny rooms thick with a haze of cigarettes and hashish. Burning lanterns also emitted a tarry smoke, and I pulled up the collar of my overcoat to protect my mouth and neck. Stagnant fluid seeped into my shoes, a toxic soup of soapy water, discarded petroleum and split plastic bottles of urine.

Home, I cleansed myself, then warmed a pan of good wine on the stove in my galley kitchen. I prepared a light grey ceramic pot with a ruby inner glaze (a gift from a sister), tucking a clean muslin cloth over the top. I retrieved the emerald from my overcoat's inside pocket and laid it gently upon the cloth. This was my self-made altar, my daily ritual for good health. As I poured the steaming wine, the smaragdus sizzled like a sauna stone. The weight of the liquid pulled the stone down into the rising red lake. I let the wine cool around the stone before draining it back into the pan to repeat the process. After three rounds of this, I took a handful of dried broad beans and pounded them in a pestle and mortar until they became a coarse paste. Then I removed the stone and muslin from the wine, and poured the paste into the pot, stirring as I went. I decanted the mixture into a flask, which I sipped throughout the day, until it was finished.

When I went to bed that night, I could breathe deeply again, the weight of the infection gone. My sinuses were clear. This is my recommendation for such thickness of mucus in the chest and head. The enriched wine has other uses too, and as I slept, I dreamed of one. I shall recount to you what followed.

II

IT WAS SHORTLY BEFORE the feast of St John the Baptist, which is to my mind a wholly pagan affair. It falls just before summer solstice, six months before the feast of Christ's birth. I was pig sick. It would have been easy to blame the seafood but I was laid up with a recurrent condition that had afflicted me since my late twenties. My gut, locked tight with cramps, was a quarrelsome animal, growling at my attempts to feed it. At times I felt well, and it relaxed while I worked, and slept while I swam. But when I rattled its cage, when my life was thrown out of balance by things outside my control, it awoke. I pushed all my anger and anxiety down beneath my diaphragm, and the beast reacted, and I can't blame it.

The heat of late June had started to bleach out the world. I lay in bed, shutters and windows wide open, and listened to the eve of the feast outside. Its main element was fire: up in the hills, bonfires burnt with sweet-smelling smoke, while inside the city walls teenagers battled with rounds of firecrackers. By night, the walls opposite were lit by incessant flashes, and my building shook with the force of the explosions. The lingering smell of gunpowder and cordite made me bilious; what I thought was another attack of chronic cramps hastened into a fever.

'*He must increase, but I must decrease*', said St John. With these words, the endless bright days became shorter. As you travel north, so I'm told, the solstice fires drive away the dark forces released by the feast.

I patted my warming brow with the first thing at hand: a cotton sock dipped in a jug of just cool water. Again I was alone – there was no one to administer any wort or unction. My room was all but empty: there was a young palm breaching its nut in the corner, a lamp on the floor beside my bed, and a junk-shop fan churning a breeze through the balcony doors. In place of a main light fitting were three wires coiling out of the plaster. I kicked the sheet to my feet and let the fever take over. I sweat into my mattress while each explosion bathed my body in their coloured light. The reverberating blasts reached my bones, and something deep within me entreated for an ill-defined salvation.

I possessed only the meagre spirituality hashed and eked out by a handful of ancestors as clumsy as I am. I knew the basics: the role of the flame, the inner light, the golden rule, the burning bush. Faith, hope, charity. I approached these notions with caution. Born in the spring, I was conceived when the sun was in the sign of Cancer. My heart has long been wracked by bad humours fleeing the liver; my stomach too. This anxious complaint and its accompanying fever have stripped back some of my comforts, since my mother and father, though not exactly humble people, gave my body and life to the city. The years that followed as a ward of the administration were never easy. The pains I felt ruined by, though barely thirty-four years of age, have been with me since that time. All of life is a gift.

I closed my eyes and asked that this fever not be the thing that consumes me, not tonight. Another firework lit from the street below flashed my bedroom a quick green. Give me something to take away the taste. I asked out loud for a doctor, and she came to me.

Let me begin with the end, just as He wrote the end when He began.

The story came to me in two parts, in two manners. Firstly, I witnessed with my body; by this I mean when I say I *saw* things, I mean I saw them, with my own outward-looking eyes. Secondly, I witnessed with my soul – that is, with my inner eyes, for with them I knew what He said. Regardless, both visions were induced in me. I recall them here; we are vehicles for stories of the other. This is what will happen in the city.

There is no way to *describe* a vision. Our mortal words are not enough to translate the mysteries of existence. When I try to describe a vision and say *I saw a dog*, for example, I do not mean to say that I *imagined* this dog, nor that I *saw* a dog, a perception. What I mean to say is *there was a dog*, inside my experience – not a mirage, but a dog whose presence I registered no less clearly than the dog that now sits at my feet. 'Vision' is an insufficient word to describe such contact with the divine; *seeing* is the smallest part of it. I write down what happened now, long after the fact, in order to explain both what I *saw* and what I *experienced*. Words are only ever signals from the experience of living and dying. Nothing I write is written to persuade you, but rather in the search for an unknown language through which to share what I witnessed with the entirety of my being. A fool's errand. Yet we persist.

I have thought for a long time about how to begin – whether from the fevered foreshadowing, or from the end, which is where it began. That is why I say, like Him, I will begin at the end. My story is a record of what happened during the last days before He created you, so you will know what to expect and how to behave. These are messages from Him. From the last days, we will go forward, from the Judgement to what came after. Those are messages from me. Imagine yourself now in the position I was then.

The city is surrounded by five mountains, or, a single range that reaches five peaks: a bowl that nature has created for the city to sit in. Green fingers of vegetation thicken towards the mountain's base with gorse and olive. The hills start at the limit of heaven and run down to the city gates, pushing at its walls, forcing its buildings, turrets, masts and towers higher as the mountain engulfs them. A city built on a city built on a city, constricted by this mountainous band; not like a shrub whose roots are bound by its pot, but like a tomato plant under a glass bell, coaxing its growth upwards. Under this glass bell, the heady climate prickles the skin of the people.

Wide boulevards for the rulers to parade along have been carved out of the ancient neighbourhoods.

Where once families sat out in the street, women washed down doorsteps, and horses and cars navigated the shady alleys, now palms, yuccas and apple trees line the central strips, and the mosaic of streaked walls has been levelled to clear the way for a grand vista. Those displaced for the boulevards moved into the old town where they live on top of each other in a dense hive. At the top of the main boulevard, a fountain floods dolphins and nymphs with fresh water drawn from springs hidden in the hills. At the bottom, an iron column rises from the old town, where I live, topped with the semblance of a man who produced power out of thin air.

Some evenings I sit on my balcony with a pomegranate juice, lightened with a little soda water, and watch the goods move along reconfigured pathways. Almonds, cooking oil, leatherwork, SIM cards, gasoline, all passed along desire lines. The city, too, was formed out of the air. The smells from the lower residences – stewing meat and spiced apricots – waft into the higher homes, which are brimming with vines and fruiting trees wherever the sun could reach.

There's little breeze within the glasshouse, which can lead you to believe that time is standing still. Life turns itself over, reproducing itself in a steady rhythm; it is not a time of crisis or upheaval, nor a time of expansion and prosperity. Yet this tomato bell is the stage for what is about to unfold.

When the day arrives, you climb to the roof of your apartment first thing in the morning, so as to enjoy a moment's peace before you go to the office. You sit back on your canvas chair, stretch out your legs, and look over the city, hearing the first cracks of pavement under the drills. The radio news drifts from a neighbour's open window, and you meditate on man's regular half-apocalypses. The movements of terrified populations, the uncontrollable fires licking the Arctic Circle, the mobilisation of many armies.

From this prone position, you are woken to the coming calamity. An ascending murmur rolls in from the five hills; it sounds like the snarling of dogs. You see these peaks every day, with loose rocks and earth betraying the constant slipping of their masses, eroded by the winds that hit the city at the start of winter. You could draw their grey skyline in the dust from memory, like the back of a sleeping lizard. Now, their familiar silhouette is broken by movement. Five beasts pace the peaks, each circling its own summit, large enough to be visible to the naked eye, and loud enough to wake still-sleeping children. The weather is fine – no stormy clouds, no claps of thunder – but five growling beasts on five peaks surround the city, stirring clouds of dust into the clear blue sky.

From a high tower behind the church spires and central city buildings, five thick ropes are tightening. As residents attend to their morning routines and perform their ablutions, you witness these ropes, sturdy enough to hold a liner to the dockside, become taut with tension above their heads. They remain unaware of the beasts, perhaps mistaking their snarling for a revving motorbike at a traffic intersection nearby. You trace the ropes' lengths with your eye as they lift over the city walls, up to the mountaintops, where they shackle the dogs. These are not coyotes, nor foxes, nor prairie dogs, hungry for carrion. They do not represent nature, whose story, we are told, is the relentless reclamation of human culture. You might be expecting an end in which nature's bloody claws scratch at the city gates as sea levels rise, as lights go out and the woods draw closer as fires choke the sky. But, at the end, the dogs arrive, not as nature's unbridled beasts – as our beasts. From their outline it seems, in fact, that they are not all dogs. They are domesticated and labouring, a companion species to ourselves. They continue to pace in circles, necks weighed down by leather collars. Five peaks, five beasts, five collars, five ropes.

The cables start to creak and moan with the strain. The tower cannot hold, you think, surely? The beasts keep pulling at the reverberating ropes, but they do not appear to want to get away. They are held fast to their mountaintops by the cables, which are pitch black, except for one, whose threads alternate between black and white, black and white, spiralled cords to the neck of the beast.

I'd like to see you do anything about this, this scene that nature has set. The rooftops now are full of people, crowded at the balustrades, as they watch the beasts set in silhouette against the morning sky. We are transfixed, but not terrified. Though these beasts are monstrous, no one seems surprised. Those of us who have stumbled home late from a liaison with a secret lover have seen them before, from the corner of our eye, as they slink from alley to alley. Our soldiers have ridden such horses. The drunk and carousing businessmen, hanging from the lampposts in the early hours, have seen the ruddy pig rootling in the sewage canals. Beasts like this don't exist in tales alone; they stalk every city, every citizen. I witness these beasts tearing at their own flesh, whose muscular strength stretched the rope tense.

The first beast I see is a fiery dog but the dog is not on fire. Imagine it before it comes. I strain to make out its features: long, gaunt, its hind quarters lifted

47

on bony joints higher than its head, face sharpened into a cruel and svelte nose. From its mouth flames burst forth, then draw back in the wind, its body like a burning torch. These licks of fire form its coat, instead of fur, covering thin ribs. It looks so hungry, I think, like a flinching addict on their last day. Have you ever seen a dog go mad? Imprisoned for too long, rabid and ravenous. The hound gnaws at itself with a concentrated passion, and I think of my fellow city dwellers who bite with territorial jealousy at every perceived encroachment on their private circles. 'This is mine and that is yours!' they snap, even though neither of us have anything. It pulls on its leash, the fire warming nothing while filling the air with acrid smoke. The environment must be choking.

The vision consumes me with sadness; I can't bear to look any longer. My eyes move to the next mountaintop, from which emanates a roar.

Above the tree line, a lion prowls, treading his wide pads on the slipping stone. More than the hound, the lion has lost any previous beauty. His tawny brown fur has been worn by time. His mane struggles from his neck. Across his body, scars criss-cross scars, bound over with the thick tissue of healing. War has drained him of life. His body is like the city walls, pockmarked from conflict, rebuilt many times. I feel a flicker of recognition: like the soul of the city, this creature may once have been bright. When it dies, will its skin peel back from its bones? Yes, I remember my mother buying tins from the market, with pictures of the leonine beast on – dead, rotting and consumed by tiny parasites, like us citizens, chipping away at the marble buildings of our ancestors. My grandfather, her father, would recount the riddle that Samson presented to the thirty Philistines at his wedding feast: *Out of the eater came forth meat, and out of the strong came forth sweetness.* I think of my grandfather, who sat on the city council, and the feasts they held.

Once, I braved myself to sneak into one, in the banqueting chamber of the City Hall. Carefully, silently, I pushed open the door to the balcony. As I did so, a great noise arose from the chamber. I tipped my head over the balcony rail to see the thirty Philistines in uproar. Silver platters scattered the long table as well as the plushily carpeted floor, flung by diners the minute their shellfish were sucked of meat, their racks of lamb chewed of flesh. Glasses brimmed with deep red wine, poured from crystal decanters, or even deeper crimson wine, tapped from kegs along the length of the table. Waiters in white waistcoats scurried to deliver plate after plate, while the men roared with laughter, gristle and vegetable cannoning from their mouths and tumblers slammed down. In the middle, roasted on a spit, a whole lion was served on a bed of roast potatoes, his stomach cut open. I stumbled back from the edge of the balcony, my stomach turning with anxious shock at the state of the men. There was no honey, only blood.

Back on the mound, the tawny lion struggles to raise his head to the sky with each roar. What would come forth from this sad king's corpse? Once a soldier, his legs lack power and his claws have been ripped from his paws. It is another sorry sight, how he paces, proud but helpless; the cruelties he had long since committed to the earth are faint memories. I imagine the men who sat at that table are all dead now too.

It would be easy to give the impression that the city is primarily a place of hard work and industry – the bustle below the higgledy-piggledy houses, the noise of the streets – but the city is a place of hedonism too. It's a contentious issue: some neighbourhoods have become embittered by the increase in revellers to the clubs and pleasure gardens. Where previously the contrast between one district and another was striking, these days they tend to bleed into one another, with the same restaurants and coffeehouses owned by the same groups of people, and their individual characters have been lost.

This is what I think when I see the third beast, a wan horse whose sinewy skin clings to her skeleton and who no longer fights to keep the flies from her face. The pleasure-seekers have not noticed; I can hear them slumbering beneath our rooftops as we watch the staggering horse struggle to hold strong under the weight of the ropes. I lower my head at this beast.

The city's rulers don't care much about these urban changes, for their coffers fill with gold faster than they can spend it. They haven't invested in basic infrastructure, despite the city's swelling numbers and the strain of the tourists, and so everything is clogging up. Traffic is heavy, and at crossroads, the fumes rise like bonfire smoke. As part of the administration, I'm aware of the privations of the populace, though I must say my department, Public Hygiene and Sanitation, is well-funded and efficient. But the drains – oh the drains! They bubble at the edges of the streets, spewing puddles of sewage that soak the trouser hems of unlucky passersby. Perhaps that's why the city's betters have their helicopters and rooftop bars, to lift themselves far from the smell.

As the beasts pace, these collected visions of the city and its people circle in my mind. The big bad dogs offer up a brazen allegory, manifestations of life's old complaints as well as of the coming death, hiding in the darkened hills. My midnight terrors have been here all along; now I can look them in the face. I've seen these howling animals before, creeping around my shoulders as I see hands run up skirts outside bars, or piggy men sniffing at underwear, or shaking their pink hands at street sellers. This collapse of public life has been coming for some time.

The fourth beast is a black boar, happy in dirt. It's smeared all over him, splashed around his nipples, coarse hair flecked with mud, and the heavy collar attached to the rope is also caked in waste. The dark pig drops his weight, rolling and snorting as he scratches his back against the rocky ground and lets the sun fall on his vast belly.

On the last hill, the last beast. A greying wolf, held by a sagging black-and-white rope, he is truly the worst of all of them. When I see him, I can't think of anything but my boss. I recognise his face in this clawed creature. Despite the fact that I am a medical doctor, he regards me as little more than a tool of social hygiene. I perform this function effectively, which means without mercy, for I well know that keeping the contagion from entering is far easier than removing the contagion once it has breached the body. He reclines at his desk with a medicinal whisky, looking over the results for my districts: what remains clean, and from within the city, and what has been found lurking, from outside the city, and what percentage of the contagion has been cleaned. He picks at his teeth with a toothpick, stroking his moustache, looking past me at two TV monitors, one of which shows switching images of the interrogation rooms in the basement, the other a building billowing with smoke. 'Look at that,' he says, without taking his eyes off the square screen, gesturing in its direction with his pick. I can make out a bit of sinew from the flesh of a cow on the end. I wonder how many people have already burned to death inside.

All the growling that woke the city this morning seemed to be coming from this last beast. He is monstrous, nearly two metres tall at his shoulders, with a shaggy mane, and his gums are showing in an evil snarl. He will take anything you hold dear, and claim it as his own, and I'd like to see you do anything about it.

All these beasts pull at their chains, their heads reaching towards the west. Like us, they will wait hungrily for the setting of the sun, for night and for death.

What a morning! The sort that fills you with hope, the way the morning sun warms the parks and infuses the city smoke with the scent of wildflowers. The sort that prompts whistling from the market traders who are arranging their goods (fruits, nuts, secondhand tools, antique lamps, kitchen equipment, aftershave, radio alarms) under the city walls. Roused by the howling, your neighbours have now joined you on the rooftop. A shuddering, silent terror creeps through the crowd. The pacing of the beasts kicks up a foul dust through which their teeth and fur emerge and recede; the air becoming ever-thicker with the smog blowing into the city, blasting the window panes and covering the windshields of morning delivery vans, forcing them to a halt. The drivers rush, coughing, to the shelter of the nearest coffeehouse or shop doorway. I cover my mouth with a rag and shade my eyes, for through the fog I sense a burning light. I am drawn to the city walls, where a light shimmers.

There, a youth sits. At first, I think, he is one of us, a citizen watching the beasts, the ropes, the whirling dust, the city's ruckus, the beating hearts. But he compels me to look closer. The youth wears a robe of purple cotton. Purple has long been a noble colour; the cost of its dyes made it prohibitively expensive in the Roman era, such that the wearing of purple was reserved for the Emperor himself. Such dyes can now be cheaply synthesised, but such an association is hard to wash out. The boy up on the city walls is arresting, not only for his classical beauty or his envied youth, but because, from the top of his unmuscled chest down to his groin, a beauteous light shines forth. So bright, it is as though the dawn rises from within the boy.

He holds a musical instrument made of two fine pieces of wood that bend in a U-shape, with a third piece covering the mouth of the U. From this, strings of catgut are stretched taut to produce a sound when plucked. He sits still upon the walls as a foil to the grotesque. You will surely remember him after what follows. He is imprinted on your retinas, he is there when you close your eyes – not only because of the powerful light that radiates from him, but because he belongs to the last time your confusion swam with curiosity, not fear.

Alas, alas, what is this? What is this that we have seen? Ach, we wretched ones, who will help us? For we do not know how we have been deceived. O omnipotent God, have mercy on us. Let us turn back, let us turn back quickly to the testament of the Gospel of Christ. For, ach, ach, ach, we have been bitterly deceived.

So the beasts, chained, and the boy, beautiful – and next, a third actor, a woman. Unlovely and unloved, she looks as though she has known much neglect as she stands there, raised above the city, plain for all to see. She is the sort of woman normally rendered invisible, unrecognised. Such uncanny figures frequent the streets and parks like automatons of the civic imagination, filling their carts with meticulously sorted trash, servicing the outgrowths of waste and abuse. In her, I see myself, in her sickness, her trembling. The woman has ditched her usual blankets of clothing to reveal to the rooftop crowds her naked body, which is covered in pustules and blisters. Her inner thighs are torn, streaked of blood, with raw ribbons of skin and a melee of yellow-black bruises. Between her legs is the most monstrous head.

I'm getting ahead of myself, with all this pornographic horror, this thrilling apocalypse. That morning on the walls, on the mountains, with the beasts, through the smog, we were shown the end of the world. To be given a vision from God is a singular blessing, yet God is no critic – it was for us mortals to interpret what this might mean.

You will recall from your studies of the Bible that I created the world in six days. On the seventh day, I rested. I hope you can understand that events can be overlaid with other meanings. When you recall that the Earth was created in six days, know also that it shall have six corresponding ages, and then, a seventh. We are here already, at the dawn of the seventh day, the Seventh Age, and I am preparing for my rest. The things I have taught you have held strong throughout the ages, though I notice that time has left my scrolls dog-eared and yellowing on the shelf. *The food of life found in the divine Scriptures is lukewarm.* So, I have turned to the latest tool to deliver this message to you. As a potter shapes clay into a vase, so I have shaped Hildegard to reveal to you the deeper secrets and mysteries of my creation and its end. The words she speaks are not her words but my words. I have put them in her mind and in her mouth.

The city is an industrious place, whether a stallholder in the central market who wraps their peaches in brown paper, or a barista who takes every effort in pouring their leaf into the foam. Work happens all year round. In the height of August, the bourgeoisie close for business to refresh themselves in their ocean-side villas outside the walls, but the rest of the citizens keep at it. I am thinking of one man in particular, a favourite of mine, who labours long hours walking in front of the street-cleaning vans. Despite his advancing years, he sweeps the cigarette ends and gravel from the pavement into the road, into the waiting brushes of the truck, which sucks the detritus up and sprays bleached water beneath its tires. When this man finishes for the day, he returns to his apartment and opens his windows. With the last rays of sun on his swollen feet, he sips from a beer so cold it has started to form crystals of ice inside the can. The cooling of the day. This corresponds to the Sixth Age, when I sent my only son to Earth to carry my Word.

I could have sent him before, but in the first five ages the people were busy enough. I sent him like the sun's incandescence at the end of the day, to illuminate the coolness of the Earth's evening, when he was most needed. I could have sent him in the Seventh Age, My words needed time to settle on the ceramic tiles, to soothe the street cleaner's feet, ahead of the Seventh Age. It gave you time to rejuvenate, to fortify yourself with faith before the sun sets and the darkness of the night fills the room, starting from the corners.

III

THE CITY'S STOMACH was upset. It struggled for collective cures. It was inevitable that such an incident would have an effect on a population. There were vigils and community leaders called to say their piece; there were radio phone-ins and marches and manifestations. Many sought out private cures. People who had previously cut contact with their psycho-therapists left messages on their voicemails, vying for a new slot, while others consulted their priests. A brave few made appointments with their physicians. A vague and common sickness prevailed, and no one was exempt. Palpitations in the night, so that when woken in the early hours by deliveries to the ground floor, people would close their balcony shutters to the outside world, despite the sweltering heat. A sense of dreadful foreboding. Bank managers received an unprecedented volume of enquiries from clients about the state of their accounts, and solicitors were overwhelmed with requests to put customers' affairs in order. To many, the resounding of church bells, once a comforting memory from childhood, became unbearable, like a fly near one's eardrum.

During the great adaptation there was a sudden urge to prepare, but no one quite knew for what. Perhaps only for the gracious and the quiet: most had spent a lifetime sorting through their spiritual documents with daily thought and deed. The rest of us were thrown into a muted frenzy. The smugglers couldn't price their cigarettes high enough. The city was even more airless than usual in the summer; it was as if the inside of our mouths were coated with cornflour and we were unable to speak. The city government had imploded, and was too busy infighting to restore itself, leaving a vacuum of reason and leadership. The city was waiting nervously, unable to interpret the significance of the messages contained in the signs I described to you in that vision. Nor were the people able to fully process the trauma of the event and its revelation, and instead continued in their sinful *omertà*.

They would not have to wait long, for it was the end of the Sixth Age. The swelter that had been building over the weeks since the beasts and the boy and the woman and the head could not be sustained. It was as though the city's heat was a ball of dough, rising in the bowl of the mountains, until it inflated over the peaks to the point of bursting. It was another stifling Sunday. Families visited their grandparents for lunch, gorging on watermelons to slake their thirst. Parents threw canvas over the orchard trees in an attempt to make shade for the children to play, so that they could retreat to back parlours to drink iced white wine. Policemen were permitted to undo two shirt buttons. That night, there wasn't a single closed window in the city, and cat burglars were unwilling to take advantage. Nobody was sleeping deeply when the storm broke, relieving as it did a thousand migraines.

It started with the joyful patter of golf-ball-sized raindrops on dry pavements and the sweet smell of dirty pollen released into the moist air. It was, at first, a soothing balm, cleansing the urine from the streets, watering flowerpots and tumbling from drain pipes, staining the brickwork like blood. The rain was so welcome that no one worried when the drains overflowed with the force to tip over mopeds and career trash cans into parked cars. But they did worry later that evening, when the rain, which had been falling in vertical sheets like heavenly curtains, was joined by a tumultuous wind. It seemed to sweep down from the directions of all five peaks, a hurricane strong enough to rip off aerials, flags, and roof tiles, to blow in doors and send chimneys crashing; to dislodge even the towers, which had stood for generations, from their foundations. Down the main boulevard where visitors would stroll, buying souvenirs and flowers and fried snacks, the kiosks were lifted above the horse-chestnuts buckling in the wind. Rivers long ago funnelled by engineers into underground sewer systems erupted, so that the boulevards became torrents, and the torrents became new rivers, racing towards the sea, which surged in turn to meet them. Still the rain fell.

The torment had not been forecast by the meteorological office. No evacuation had been considered. The moment had come for time to come to an end.

The five mountains that just weeks earlier had harboured those beastly augurs disintegrated like sandcastles in an encroaching tide. The elements broke open, broke free, to unleash all the energy they had ever held upon the world. Everything that was once considered immutable – from the city and the weather to time, thermodynamics, and love – all were to be transformed.

The Holy Occupation arrived with the loudening sound of a falling bomb. Everything was subsumed to the power of the occupying authorities. Everything mortal, everything that lived and drank and sinned, was dissolved in the deluge just as a handful of salt dissolves in a boiling pot of pasta. When the purifying waters receded, the land, we can assume, was well salted.

No occupation can succeed without collusion. Sectors of the population were identified that might find common cause with the Heavenly Army of God. They were the dead, and the salted earth gave them back to their maker. Flesh was returned to their bones, muscles and tendons wrapped around joints, the network of each nervous system relit with electric connections. In the blink of an eye, the dead were reanimated, even after limbs lost in threshers or skulls cracked beneath tyres. The drowned, nibbled at by fishes; the lost, devoured by wolves – all sprung to life, sprouting hairs and accumulating fat, ready to walk among the living. Written on them are the records of their former lives: the good radiated goodness, while the bad couldn't be washed clean. The time had passed for them to make amends.

The dark clouds that had brought the hurricane winds continued to threaten above. Below, citizens

63

prepared to flee the pandemonium wrought by the resurrected dead in advance of the weather. What lay behind the stormy front was unknown, and the population's mood was certainly not one of curiosity. Their hurry was futile, for Christ the Administrator, who held total executive power of the occupied lands, was soon to arrive. His long-prophesied presence had not been what the citizens had expected. Carving up what remained of the city into manageable zones, he was earthly enough to understand the ways of the world, the corruption of humans, and as such implemented a pitiless system of drumhead justice. What had previously passed for the law would no longer suffice under this new regime, for laws can be bent to fit. No, the divine government would arrange things according to justice, and Christ the Administrator had already been taking names.

The new courts opened swiftly. Summons were issued to the whole citizenry, living and undead alike, and the seats were packed with the population of heaven, hell and earth. The atmosphere was that of a bow drawn across a single violin string, reverberating with the timbre of judgement. There was no bench for a jury, nor desks for advocates, because judgement had been tied up for so long before this day there was no need for argument. Even those accused already knew whether they would be found guilty or innocent as they stood in contemplation of their fate. The long-winded session was solely for the benefit of the spectators, for whom there were plenty of surprises: certain esteemed doctors and priests, with their private practices and fundraising dinners, received among the severest public punishments.

Before the Administrator lay generous wreaths of flowers, symbolic of those who were to be rewarded. There were begonias for the patriarchs and prophets, on whose teaching the city had built its foundations. There were lilies to honour the apostles, who had helped the Administrator with his work. For the martyred and their confessors there were dahlias, and for the virgins and widows, pink and white orchids. For the good monarchs who mortified their flesh for the administration, there were red poppies. And above all of these buds, rolling from the dais on which he stood, there were plumes of bougainvillaea, in honour of those who considered this world to be nothing; who said: '*This life is more glorious than that.*'

Meanwhile, the prisons, whose walls had been broken open by the catastrophic storm, gave up their inmates for their second judgements. Delivered before the warm hand of justice rather than the punitive arm of the law, out in the holy state they saw their status turn. The city's penal code was overturned and ex-convicts watched their correctional officers dragged down while they were on their way up.

While some had feared the Day of Judgement's terror, and others had awaited its quenching right-eousness, few could have predicted how entertaining His reckoning would be.

On the mountainside to the north of the city, a more terrible punishment was beginning. There, the unfaithful and indecent, the polluted, were gathered by the administration. The Devil lurked among them. They looked back into the city – once their welcoming home – to see the wreckage, the proceedings, the quiet enactment of His Word. They saw the court in session and sighed with regret, for they knew they wouldn't be afforded the luxury of having their case heard. Christ the Administrator had already arranged their swift dispatch into hell.

The final authority of the heavens had made itself manifest. There was no need for the city any more: not for the bustle of the marketplace, the heat of the nightclub, nor the roar of the crowd. The advancing front, all wind and water, had destroyed the city in its entirety. The clouds retreated, and in their wake was nothing. The site was declared clean of filth and corruption; henceforth, it was a flat plain. At times, fire burned there with gleaming intensity. The air, fresh from the ocean, was crystal clear without the wood smoke and diesel fumes. The water collected in still pools. The sun stopped turning, it was always midday – not that there was anyone left to enjoy it. All sensual pleasures were at last overcome. From then on, in the state of God, there was simply the constant sunshine of cloudless divinity.

PART II

PART II

IV

SICKNESS MAKES a foreign country of you. Isolated and without language, I turned over in bed to see myself in the mirror, but I didn't recognise this stranger. As sweat began to form on my skin and I became more helpless, I felt less ashamed of turning to her in my dreams and asking for help. I wasn't, as far as I could tell, alone, but the body beside me was not mine. I pressed a finger to my arm to feel for a vein; the sensation of blood pumping, felt through the finger, also pumping blood, is eerie to me, unbodied. The fingerprint leaves its impression, a white island within the burning red.

In truth, the city was far from eradicated. Prophecies prove inaccurate. Even an occupying authority cannot totally erase a centuries-old urbanity from the map. Or rather, the city may disappear from the map, but in memory the territory holds hard, too hard to ever dissipate. For the people, it will last as long as they do, and there were plenty of citizens left. In the months that followed, we saw both a return to normality – meals needed to be made and babies delivered – and a slow reorganisation of the way the city functioned.

The limits of the Holy Occupation reached only to the new city walls, ramparts hundreds of years old ('new' was a relative term), the masonry reinforced and repaired as they reached upwards. The City of God was manifest, the gates locked, and order was gradually returning through the judicial contagion. It was clear that the initial assessments were vastly over-optimistic: resistance was tougher and more insidious than expected. Sin was not just a way of life but a mode of being for most of the population. Part of me felt a degree of sympathy for the occupiers; they were now in the position our department had been in for years, fire-fighting systemic problems, while increasing frustration resulted in greater brutality. But the same casual attitude towards sin betrayed a helpful characteristic in the people: they were malleable to change.

My offices were closed immediately. Or rather, they failed to open. I assume many, if not most, of the central administrative building's staff were taken in the first strike. The subsequent sweeps would have picked up most of the rest, aided by a slew of willing informers with axes to grind and grudges against the former regime.

Moments of revelation are brief and ecstatic, freeing the realm of imagination, of possibility. This revolutionary fervour is better known as lawlessness. It is at first euphoric, because the wildest ideas can prosper and new forms can be applied to all relations, now unencumbered. But no revolution clears away existing forms entirely. Instead, they breed malignantly, as though the old ways had deprived them of oxygen and they are released to the wind. They are parasitic on past bitterness. Even – or especially – the most utopian people clash with contagions. And so it was that God's most conscientious snitches had lists pressed into his cold left hand within hours.

At night, I heard cries. Their sharp, persistent sound made me remember a demonstration of truck drivers, back in a time of pressing political crisis. Normally the quiet workers, who pressed through the hinterlands in the darkness to deliver the fresh produce that would appear magically on stalls by

73

morning; for their protest, they ground to a halt and pounded their horns. If a single horn produced a spritely parp, collectively they culminated in an unbearable cacophony, the kind that carried over the rooftops and up stairwells through your vibrating fingertips and down your spine. 'Dignity' was what they had scrawled on their truck banners.

These night-time cries belonged to the tortured. When the noise of the re-emerging street activities – half-commerce, half-crime – had died out for the evening, the baying began to rise from the basements. The sounds of pain and undelivered mercy were carried on the evening breeze. Each wail combined with the next in a softly penetrating drone.

I know not what they were trying to extract – confession, details of the civic administration, repentance, or all three – but each night, as I tried to drop off to sleep, I felt certain that I could recognise certain voices, baritone or with peculiar pitch, and feared for the old friend, colleague or comrade who had been picked up in a sweep. It was a devilish fear, experienced no doubt by everyone, even the snitches (or especially them). The terror came from both the imagination of the action that caused each yelp, and the acknowledgement that you could be the next to bleed.

Angels worked these torture chambers and patrolled the streets. They could be seen descending from the flaming sky, wings glittering with a thousand blinking eyes that reflected the light of heaven onto the darkened city. Their sparkle was but a prelude for the cruelty they were about to enact. I would close off the lamp in my kitchen and stand in front of the window to see them drift down like falling pollen dropped by suffocating clouds.

Yes, I previously worked within the city administration. Even when judged against the new regime, this bureaucratic body has a reputation for unethical behaviour, corruption, and, to an extent, cruelty – although I feel like these allegations fade in light of the later brutalities. As I saw it, we ran a system that prioritised those who, actively or passively, believed in order as the beating heart of any civilised achievements. Outside the city walls was evidence enough of life without administration: beyond the farming colonies that stretched into the fertile valleys of the hinterlands were areas of banditry and battles, malarial swamps, incestuous fortified homesteads, sickness and insurrection. In the wake of droughts and floods, these subversive scenes were left over, remnants of a once Christendom. And why did we need to stretch our farming lands further down the long valleys, fed by highways and railroads, taming that rough land? Because each year more and more of the outsider inhabitants would appear at our gates, demanding safety and security, wanting a claim to prosperity and civilisation. It was our duty and honour to provide the liberty of a free city, and it was our responsibility to ensure the stable basis for such a life.

Any mother knows that her children's hands must be clean before they sit at the dinner table; this mother is not one who holds their dirty fingers beneath scalding and soapy water, no matter how often the little brutes may call her a tyrant. Likewise, my pens and paper, with their efficient instructions, were the scrubbing brush and the suds, the surgeries and the medical vans, the bleach and the chlorine – you understand. My time in the service was not therefore something I looked back on regretfully.

The new regime had little time for clean hands. They needed no hygienic chemicals. 'Sunlight is the best disinfectant,' we used to hear from the City Hall; a fallacy to a medical professional such as myself, though I appreciated the metaphorical power. Well now they had all the sunlight they could wish for, and more. From the thousand eyes of the Angels, ultraviolet rays could blister skin and fill the trenches grooved in the hillside with fire. Just as your watch was on the verge of fusing to your flesh, the ice-cold wind abruptly blew. Worse, the overpowering fumes from the burning trenches of bodies incapacitated thought. Knowledge seeped from the flesh, experience atrophied like the skin on your bones. We moved in a sheep-like stupor, in obedient response to this obedient terror.

I am hardly free of sins of judgement. I will not go into the details here. It is enough for me to suggest that the prior administration's pursuit of social hygiene was utilitarian to the point of making judgements that were perhaps not ours to make. To put it another way, we expanded the concept of the pest to ever-larger carriers of contagion. What came over, under or through the city walls was immediately suspect; the city was clean, the land was not. Radiological and biological decontamination, delousing and sterilisation were the public face of our operations. I interpreted my Hippocratic Oath within the logic of the wider social body. I, and the city in which I lived, did not live in a state of grace. At that point, I was unaware of quite what my status would be under the new guard.

Yes, I fully expected the knock on the door and, yes, I recognised the echo of irony from the hundreds of doors I had ordered to be knocked. Perhaps there *is* such a thing as divine retribution, I thought. I spent my nights contemplating not only my potential losses, but those of the women who I filtered through our program. If I were to be taken, I would leave nothing behind, looking back only on a prison open to the heavens. The women, however, could see tantalising glimpses of past joys all around, through their black lace veils during Holy Week, or as they raised their eyes from their imposed doorstep-washing routines. Now, we lived in an uneasy settlement. After the first few attempts to get back to my offices, I stayed largely at home, heading out for rations with a scarf covering my face at dusk, whose bruise-dark half-light provided a better disguise even than darkness, as it distorted your features with shadow.

I lived just outside of the old city wall, in one of those peculiar districts bound to its inhabitants by psychology and history. Upon the old wall's obsolescence, my neighbourhood had been repurposed by the poor as a favela. When I was a child, it developed into somewhere neater, with shuttered window frames and compact, well-stocked shops. Before the occupation, I would walk home from my offices in the central administrative district, down these bustling, covered streets, stopping to buy a few fried aubergine slices to tide me over until I would meet my sisters for dinner, or to visit a stationers for a refill for my ink pen. These shops had been staffed since my childhood by people who seemed to have grown like trees inside their crowded walls. They fit the space so naturally, arms reaching to the limits of the shelves, from which they would bring down whatever you wanted: wax candles wrapped in brown paper, tins of preserved fish, religious books in every language on Earth.

You would think the forest of traders would stand forever, but the occupation authorities stumped them. In the name of public health, the whole street was shuttered and layers of graffiti were pasted over with official notices. 'Sure it's vermin they're after,' the wizened greengrocer muttered to me from the closed entrance of the market bar. 'Or rather, rats . . .' They wanted to limit the supplies of rations, to ensure any dissenters of Holy Law would be starved out of their holes. His eyes fastened on mine, and I wondered whether I too would be ratted out, and what price the catcher would get for me.

My apartment had survived the siege, although my bedroom walls were streaked with sulphurous dust. My sickness, nursed from the times of the peace, would not recede as long as I slept in this blackened tomb. My nights were agonising. The physical pain was just one component of my misery. My stomach felt more alienated from the rest of me than ever before. It harboured all my anxieties and fear about the future. I went to bed in an airless panic, sleeping fitfully with a fast heartbeat and high blood pressure. The only communication I received from God was in the form of orders for present obedience. Everything to come was unknown. What level of terrible would this administration reach?

I had heard word that in the administrative district they were starting to piece together what had once been the bureaucracy of the civic administration, by then a bitter, unspoken memory. When I woke up in the night, I would stare from my balcony at the ruins. A few brick buildings stood half intact, but most had been brought down to piles of stone atop their cellars. A few survivors had managed to dig into these cellars for shelter; there was an occasional flash of lamp or head torch, or a glow when the wooden door covering the entrance to the hollow was opened to let in a returning scavenger. The strings of smoke that rose from these hovels recalled the books I read as a child, as if at the foot of some fallen tree a little mouse family were warming themselves before their stove in their hidey-holes. But their inhabitants weren't mice, they were human beings, trapped between this life of bare survival and the possibility of torture and fire. From my sixth-floor apartment I looked across this ruined cityscape, where a powerless army of citizens had somehow trodden through the wreckage along the same paths as the old street plan. I was surprised to find myself wishing the angelic occupiers had been bold enough to rethink the city a little more efficiently.

It came, eventually, the knock. Although it wasn't what I had prepared for, with my triple-locked door and hammer and knife on the hallway table. In fact, it wasn't a knock at all. It happened one evening when I was slinking down the stairwell, lights switched off, all quiet. I reached the last step and was fumbling for my key in the marble-cold lobby when I felt a strong draft blowing in from behind me. Discarded take-away leaflets, dry leaves and cigarette ends – all rushed up around me. The dark catalysed into intense white heat like the flame of magnesium salts, throwing my shadow against the door. Light bounced around illuminating the hall, its cracked pipes and dirty tiles. I buried my face into my elbow crease, and through my flesh could almost feel the bones of my joints, pushed hard together. It was as if the space had become a vacuum, and now the force was spinning upwards like a tornado. My feet left the linoleum and there I hung, as if from a meat rack. The sucking of the air died down and the blinding brightness dimmed somewhat. I dropped my arm and opened my eyes.

Two gigantesque creatures of a heavenly presence moved before me. Still I hung. There is no language to adequately describe the sight of these creatures. From the shoulders down they burned with a light of imperceptible magnificence. They were here on behalf of the new authority, the first of the last armies of Angels, belonging to the second highest rank of the choirs, which we knew as cherubim. They were the most fearsome wing of the intelligence corps, known for their brutal efficiency: a set of eyes in every home, street, supermarket and workplace. They were the knock from which all citizens recoiled. Their faces were human and handsome. They held me floating at their eye level, to inspect me, ensuring they had their quarry. When they lowered me to the ground I tried to stand upright, but found no strength in my limbs. My legs buckled like those of a newborn foal, and within me my sense of self withered before their light.

As you progress through life, you build up a cohesive identity step by surprise step. By our thirties, our achievements speak for us, like fine leather brogues or our choice of cigar. Each new worker under your command, every new district cleansed and running efficiently, contributes to your sense of purpose. My work made me who I am, or who I was; it gave me purpose and granted me respect. A strong young woman, I felt I operated beyond the power of most men's control. I wanted to architect my destiny. Is that supposed to be *bad*? To be autonomous and self-sufficient?

Yet before the Angels, what was I? They already knew my role, my responsibilities, my history and capabilities. That is why they were there, to interrogate me. Before their statuesque bodies I slumped to the floor. Their insight penetrated and I grew smaller.

Their voices were colossal yet soundless, rippling my body with a cosmic reverberation. Rising above both were a pair of feathered wings, not white like in the movies but black like a crow's at the top, gradating to shimmering grey at the bottom. On each feather was a human eyeball, puffed out from its socket. As I lay flat on the floor, every eye turned to look at me in scrutiny. Pinned in the gaze of these unearthly creatures, I soiled myself; a further humiliation, as if there was no part of my being they couldn't see.

The eyes shivered in synchrony, as though caught briefly in a breeze; then, their pupils shifted from bright blue to silver. Each eye became a mirror, reflecting my terrified visage back at me as I attempted to stand up. There was nothing left of me; I was no longer a doctor nor a citizen; I had been reduced to a body, a body sapped of strength. How, I wondered, had anyone withstood their power long enough to endure this? Perhaps I was not as strong as my old adversaries, those wards of the state onto whom I exerted my care. Perhaps those women saw in the mirrors their children and families, their histories and beliefs. I saw nothing but my weak flesh, and I only hoped the Angels would see something worth redeeming, to give me a trial rather than the summary deliverance downwards.

The mirror-eyes peered with further intensity. The features of a thousand human faces, brows furrowed in pensive judgement, emerged from within their silvered orbs. A citizen's jury. I lay paralysed in fear. I knew what they had come for. In their gaze I saw a holy love – a love that forgives unrepented indiscretions, those thoughts and deeds committed but not redeemed. Not an earthly love that loves for love in return. Not a love borne of base desires, which swims and is spent in bodily fluids, evaporating in the night air to fall as dew in the dark streets. No, a true and just love that is not afraid to search, to ask questions and pursue answers. There were many answers that the Angels of the first-final army hunted within me – questions regarding guilt, mine and others', questions regarding the acts of the administration. Punishing questions that raised in me an impossible, undisguis-able guilt, for I too had perpetrated crimes against the people. We all wrestle with the Devil inside, and we are driven to absolve ourselves of feelings of guilt. That piss-filled stairwell became a confessional in which, without words, my heart admitted all my sins and gave over my secrets to the thousand faces.

Within all of us should remain a single question: Do you believe in the light?

The question stays within me, and to have the question is enough, for through this inquiry work can be done. It is only when the question of the truth of the light has been extinguished that there is no hope. As the Angels' wings stretched higher against the confines of the stairwell, sprinkling plaster on me, I could do nothing but offer up my battles as proof that the question still lived within me. With that admission, my interrogation came to an end.

The burning light of the Angels again surged forth before disappearing with the same rush of air with which it arrived. My eyes tried and failed to adjust to the darkness; as far as I was aware, I had been struck blind. I lifted myself from the floor, each joint in pain as though attacked by gout, and followed my muscle memory back up the staircase. Once inside my twilit apartment, horror pulled at my flesh as I collapsed on the low sofa, wrapping a woollen blanket around my shoulders. Every passing light, every creaking floorboard, every distant explosion, every sobbing widow – all triggered my heart to race.

I knew they would be back. I held too much useful information to be discarded into flames. My spiritual testimony that night had delivered me from the immediate judgement taking place in the pits outside the city. Next time, would another, more brutal tier of the heavenly choirs arrest me – perhaps the fifth army with their unyielding armour, who, after forcibly extracting knowledge, would discard my emptied body?

For the rest of the night, the questions turned over in my head. Did I have the light within me? Had I left undone those things I ought to have done? Was I happy? Was I just? And the hardest of all: Was I good?

Was the light still within me? Yes – I had no doubt that I still asked myself the question, and so there was a chance that something of my experience was salvageable. Yet I could not balance any of these thoughts with the idea that the intolerable tortures of the occupation were part of a higher plan. If it came to it, could I allow myself to be put to work for this cruel judgement? Eventually, I retreated from the cold sofa to my iron-framed bed.

V

WHAT POPULAR UNDERSTANDING of the catastrophe emerged during the occupation? I attempted to discern how others in the semi-judged city tried to make sense of this sea change. I was impressed, I shall admit, with their fortitude. When I had worked for the Health Administration we had regarded the proletariat as instrumental if docile actors, whose function within the city was largely guided by the structure and order we provided. As a public hygienist, operating on the lowest ranks, I gave the regime its finishing shine. Who came before me but those whom the centrifuge of our social system had failed to draw in, poor wretches thrown outwards yet still bound by the city walls. When I ventured out into the occupied city to join the people's queues for bread, soup and manna, and overheard their whispered accounts of survival under this regime, it began to dawn on me that, far from docile, the population were of notable resilience. I hid what I could of myself and spoke little, trying to glean what I could of the news they exchanged, weighing up the conflicting rumours of righteous torment, alert to any meagre hope from what they spilled as they ate.

The nearest food store and kitchen to me had been established in a former sports centre in a paved public square. In front of the building stood a single column that held a crucible on top, in which a flame used to burn. Extinguished during the first of the last days, the bowl now sat full of cinders. When I was released from my strict seminary outside the walls, and sent into the city to start my career of service, I would come to the square often. It wasn't classically beautiful – none of the architecture or equine sculptures of the central squares were. There was no showy formality, no close observation like I had been raised with in the state seminary, no pressure for faith, responsibility and patria. Here I could sit with my sandwiches on my lunch break, as if I were just another office girl, reading the paperback novels I bought from the dark-blue kiosk. The news vendor had commented that my tastes were unusual: I chose historical fiction and detective thrillers, while most young women my age (I was no more than nineteen when I arrived for my first posting) would buy romances, so he said. It would never have occurred to me that such encounters, which I had only heard about in hushed words between students' beds, could be committed to paper, yet alone published. I began to buy the romances to try to acclimate myself to the life of a city girl, but their ruses never made much sense to me. The girls were so flighty, so trim and malleable to the expectations of the hapless men. I soon went back to my thrillers, looking up between chapters to see the city people going about their days, and the teenagers gathering outside the sports centre with duffle bags of gym kit.

After the inferno, the cypress trees lining the square's outer edges had been stripped of leaves. Angels stood either side of the sports hall's gates, their thousand eyes upon the two long queues for food that snaked through the white ash. The Eyes, they had come to be called, on account of their broad, surveilling wings, like divine peacocks. The newsstand was chained shut, the news vendor's stool upturned and legless beside it. A few families had set up a makeshift market of looted goods, silverware, vases, and the like.

Who were they kidding? Even if any of us had money, we had no future to furnish. Even the finest furniture from the homes of the rich, who had been judged or delivered already, or left for dead in their cellars, mouths stuffed with the socks they were wearing that day – even the mahogany dressers and upholstered chaises longues – were worth only their weight as firewood. And why haul an armoire back when slow-burning ceiling beams and doors lay pre-broken and piled in the rubble? Commerce was nothing more than a conditioned instinct, a habitual imagination. To see anyone browsing the flea-market tables, upturning crockery for hallmarks, was a fiction; to see anyone handing over coins to take them home was a madness.

But then madness was the order of the day. In the following weeks, some evolved from our ranks into madhouse theologians and conspiracy theorists. They began by explaining their ideas about *how this came to be* within the queues, and they entranced their audience. As their popularity grew, these self-elected preachers did not stand in line, but mounted the muddy flower-beds to hold forth and further their visions. Most were harmless enough, encouraged by the desperate and the credulous, who would return from the degrading examination that preceded the doling out of food, and offer up a tithe of meagre rations to the preachers.

The ones with the rosiest stories would return to their shelters loaded with produce, gifted by grateful housewives hungry for a taste of hope. The Angels saw them grifting and let them stay. Their judgement would come and they would be judged.

At first I recognised the preachers when they popped up, but as they blended into the new ways of the city, I began to suspect that some were not simply lay people with a popular message. Their message of subservience and justice seemed too slick, their celebration of the martial virtues and the conquering spirit too conformist, too useful. I began to suspect the hands of the Angels in all preachers. One in particular caught my attention, with the charred cypresses as his backdrop through the bitter mist and a circle of apostles surrounding him, carrying between them a crude axe and a banner. On the banner was painted a disembodied hand, two fingers curled and two straight in the sign of benediction. Even from my place in the line, which moved as usual at a crawl around the perimeter of the square, I could hear his proselytizing words. There is no doubt he was charismatic, persuasive even. This, he told us, was not the greatest catastrophe, but the purification, the cleansing. Before the curious pack of rationees, he had hit on something: our sense of interminable stasis. Even those of us who had predicted the imminent end had expected a sharp severance between before and after. This limbo, our processing put on hold, our punishments deferred, was almost more dreadful. This was the queue for eternity.

This preacher, I learned, went by the name Bernhard, and he brought to the gathered something even the fear of God had not offered: resolution. His smiling mouth offered a refrain heard since the sibyls, a prophecy unwound. This was not the end, but an interregnum. 'Take solace in your servitude, for the damned have left and we are the elect,' he boomed. I've heard this, I thought. I've heard this all before. I recognised his arch tones, his pseudo-poetry that grabbed its listener by the neck and throttled them to the ground. This Bernhard, I realised, had been present in my days of education, lecturing on state management, agriculture and hygiene. At night, his metal-capped boots pacing the corridors kept us awake, lest he stop outside our two-girl dorm.

How had he escaped punishment, I wondered? How had he evaded judgement for this hunger for power, this pursuit of authority through fear?

Bernhard knew two truths: service and war, service and war. He had spent his life waging war on filth, and in doing so, he had risen to the most severe, the most formidable administrator within the service. His was an iron fist without a velvet glove, gripping the populace. Alive, and already turning himself to the service of new Angels, God must have made a mistake.

I hurried home that morning, without even my usual passing thought for the fond news vendor of before. Bernhard wouldn't remember me, but I covered my face as I swept past his DIY pedestal, from which he sent forth his words on the elect and the justice of God into the crowd – 'A thousand-year reign and a final paradise . . .' As I turned the corner, my unleavened bread tucked beneath my overcoat, I spotted – for the first time since the first last day – an acquaintance.

Her name was Miss H. She was young, maybe ten years my junior, in her early twenties. She had been part of the typing pool in the offices, a group of junior secretaries who circulated as needed between minor officials such as myself when we had reports to compile. Fraternising was in general frowned upon, to protect the young ladies from the more powerful men in the department who might, in the words of the administration, corrupt them. Miss H. had been assigned to me on three occasions the previous year. She was fastidious, hardworking, and I had appreciated her reflections. We struck up a conversation about work, and before long we realised we had been trained in the same institution. Her hair sat in high curls, and she brought an unusual cheer to my office. For me, friendship was a rare stone in a fast-moving stream. I can't say Miss H. was my friend, but I can say I looked forward to her company. And I knew Miss H. knew the system – which others one might feasibly make friends with, and so on – whereas the ladies in my apartment building didn't understand.

To see Miss H. then, repacking her rations in her canvas bag, was a shock. I hadn't dared imagine the warmth of recognition; the conditions of our exist-ence foreclosed security in relationships and anything resembling continuity with life before. A thrill that she had survived, that anyone like her could survive in this hostile environment. A hope. She didn't notice me, I don't think.

I continued along by the shuttered bus depot, looking over my shoulder for Eyes. I checked the coast was clear and snuck in, dropping close to the floor so that my shadow could not be seen through the windows, but I could still get a clear view of the street through the gap in the door. This was irrational. The mirror-eyes must have clocked me. Yet a nagging intuition compelled me to wait there, with hands in my armpits for warmth, and sure enough, after an hour or so, I saw Miss H.'s hooded silhouette walk past.

Some force, perhaps a primal longing for human contact sent me after her, and this time I stepped out without even checking the road, until I was four or five metres behind her. She was so close, but she could disappear again at any minute. And so I hissed – I couldn't give away her name. She quickened her pace, and I hissed again, then called out: 'Hey!' She shot a glance back as her body propelled forwards. After looking behind her once more, she seemed to pause in fright, and then stepped into the doorway of the next shop. As I approached, her hand reached out and bundled me in with her.

She didn't embrace me, as such. She clung to the collars of my overcoat, her forearms pressed against my chest. She stared me straight in the eyes a moment of intimacy we had never shared, nor perhaps had I ever shared. 'You're alive,' she said. Yes, I'm alive, I thought. And so are you. We stood together in the furtive doorway, and she repeated, 'You're alive. I'm so glad you're alive.'

My tongue struggled to form words after so long mute. 'Where are you living?' I stumbled. Her neighbourhood destroyed, she was staying on the other side of the city . She had come to this rationing centre because she thought that no one would recognise her. I felt guilty, or glad, that her paranoia was stronger than mine – guilty, because I was surely higher up on the Angels' lists, and glad, that she had such foresight, to keep herself alive. 'Come,' I told her, 'I live near.'

Climbing the stairs, she was out of breath by the time we reached my door, and I unlocked the many locks that kept my place secure. Inside, I relocked them, and by the time I had done this she had found herself a seat in the lounge. I had taken to building my evening fire there, using my old bathroom door to block the light that would leak onto the street, while allowing the draught from the back of the apartment to push the smoke out. I still had some fuel for my cooking stove, and offered to boil her some water. I looked at her face again, and was struck by a deep sense of gratitude that I no longer held rank over her.

'I have a stock cube,' I said to her. 'I would like to share it with you.'

She broke into a shy smile. 'Thank you, I would like that, a lot.'

As the water came to a simmer, I dropped in the cube from its waxed paper wrap. It frothed upon contact and the room was filled with its salty smell. I stirred the broth with a fork to break up the last bits, then poured it into two enamel cups. Her lips turned red as the hot liquid touched them. We each broke off a small piece of our bread.

We sat in silence, either side of the dwindling furnace, as the weak winter sun dropped below the city's broken-down walls. As the light faded, the streets were dimly lit by the glow of the fire pits still being fed on the hillside. The peripheral massacre reflected in the embers of the stove. When the wind changed, the pungent smell would rise into my apartment, the screaming carried by the twilight air. What words could address this situation? I held out my hand and she clasped the tips of my fingers.

'Are you coping?' I asked her, wondering what knowing might change.

'Well, yes,' she said. 'I haven't *seen* that much. I was inside the offices when it began, and then I left immediately for my husband's family home.' I didn't know she was married. Perhaps I had assumed that she was like me, devoted to the service. What she could know of me, she knew of my service to the Health Administration, and to know of my service was to know all of me. It seemed so strange for us to have passed through that formation only to end up back where we would have been, had we never been volunteered as orphans of the state. I let my hands slip until our fingers were barely touching.

'I was right to leave,' she said, without taking her eyes off the flames. 'Only a few were lifted right away, but I've heard how they came, still come. The typists . . . I've met some in the lines, and they say the Angels are picking us up one by one. Shaking us down for info. Then they disappear. I can't help but wonder . . .' She finally caught my eye. '. . . but I think we know.'

I knew many had been taken initially, but this information was my worst fear, given my recent visitors. She moved her fingertips across my palm and wrist, trailing up my forearm, where they came to a rest. An electric anxiety rushed through my nervous system, tempered, only just, by the softness of her hands against the thin layer of fat by my elbow. 'I'm glad they haven't taken you.' I surged to my feet.

'We need some more heat. I will light a proper fire. You can't leave now, the streets will already be full of banditry. Stay here.'

'No, I should go, my father-in-law will be waiting.' I found this response curious, and couldn't tell whether this meant her husband was away, dead, or judged. I felt sure she should stay, for her own sake, not only to assuage the wave of loneliness that had flooded the easeful solitude I usually felt at home.

'Really, it is not safe. I have seen the risks from this very window. We can walk you back in the morning.' She weighed it over in her mind. 'Please. I would never forgive myself,' I continued. She nodded in acceptance.

I tore some pages from one of the books piled by the doorway and began to light the promised fire.

'Thank you,' she said, then pulling from inside her jacket a tin of fish, 'we can eat this.'

As the fire burned we discussed a little of the past, of working at the Health Administration, and she told me about her husband, how they had met in a nightclub, and how his family welcomed her despite having so little. Like those queueing for bread, and like our peers in the H.A., she was, above all, adaptable.

'Have you planned an escape?' she asked. I was stunned. Slipping away had not crossed my mind. 'Escape? How . . . how do you mean? I mean, where would I go? The hinterlands are already occupied – there's nowhere to escape *to*.'

'Granted,' she said. 'The hinterlands are a barrier – but only a barrier. I heard that Bernhard has been enlisted by the authorities because people are missing. At the shelter we stay in, sometimes in the night while we are asleep, or pretending to be, I hear people leaving, sneaking out. They are not lifted, not saved, not judged. The rumours are there is another place. This life, this city, is not all there is. There are places beyond His reach.'

'This is preposterous, Miss H. I worked higher up than you in the H.A. and we never heard of this. Never.'

'Look, I have never escaped, so I can't vouch for it. We could never all get out. But if the hinterlands can be traversed, someone could . . .'

'These are the fictions of prisoners. No, this is a fantasy,' I corrected. 'A salve to our waiting. Suddenly, in the moment of judgement, a new city?'

'Not so. My husband talked about this place long before, long before the last days. It was common knowledge, or a common rumour, among our type. Perhaps that's why you've never heard, you know . . .' She looked around at my flat, which despite the sooty darkness showed diminished signs of my former status. 'It's not the sort of rumour you'd share with your superiors. But I heard girls in the typing pool mention it. They said that things happen differently there.'

'Is that what they say?'

'Yes, they say that no one is wealthy, so if no one is, then what's the problem? And they're not tarnished there. It's a republic. The Tafur Republic.'

'But I have never heard of the Tafur people. I would have heard of such a race, I am sure. I never encountered anyone in the H.A. It sounds like a fiction.'

'Not a race,' she countered, 'an idea. They are a people who have chosen to be together. In their poverty, they are righteous. They are not kind, perhaps, not cultured like us, but they are feared and respected.'

I dismissed Miss H. and her talk of the Tafurs once again. We settled down on blankets beside the last of the fire, aware of the Angels overhead, whose piercing light crept around the edges of the blanket covering the window.

The next morning I walked Miss H. back to her shelter along the back streets, the two of us huddled like vagrants. We didn't make any arrangements to see each other again. She knew where I lived, I guess, and I her, but the intimacy we had shared that night came to be as I imagine so many were under the Holy Occupation. With little chance for safe discourse, such covert exchanges were easy to overplay. You could fall into a sense of false intimacy whenever fleeting moments of proximity, of friendship, were snatched. I felt ashamed by my thoughts the previous night and made no effort to search her out again.

Yet what she had told me of the Tafurs, of a poor, open city, stayed with me. Perhaps it did exist, this place of the disenfranchised, or perhaps it was the office workers' overactive imaginations. Here I was, having lost my position and purpose, drawn back to the idea that over the hinterlands was a Tafur Republic, which apparently evaded the judgement of the Lord. I wondered how they had maintained the dream of this invisible, vivid city, and whether I too could access it, as a reality more than a vision.

VI

THE ANGELS HAD LEFT ME to consider my fate. I returned to my rituals of asking beyond for guidance as to what would come next. The expectation of my inevitable seizure made me crazy over the ensuing weeks. It drove me away to somewhere else, anxiety transforming into flight, but this impetus for movement was held back by counter-worries – about leaving my comforting castle, and moving into the absolute unknown. I had no idea what lay on the other side of the ruins, nor how long I had left.

It was almost two months later when my hand was forced. I was waiting in line at the ex-post office, now a labour bureau. Here the occupation forces would recruit citizens for menial tasks: sorting through electrical goods for rare-earth metals, loading and unloading trucks . . . I was there with a false pass I had attained from a shyster in my building, a hoarder of gasoline and oxygen cans, staples of the black market. There had been talk of upped rations that day, for those who were employed, and I needed something to satisfy my aching guts.

A squad of Angels walked by the line. The rations could wait. I had no will to hand myself over to the holy authority. I tightened the straps of my rucksack so it sat high on my back and beat a retreat down the side street. I saw an Angel up ahead, and the Angel saw me, and knew me.

A few hundred metres further in front there was a scuffle; four Angels had swooped down on a man who was, I am certain, unclean, and whose papers were out of order. As the man was blessed by The Eyes, I bolted under the cover of his screams. I made it away, I thought, unnoticed, but as I darted for a doorway in the intersecting street, another Angel turned towards me, eyes glinting.

I ducked down behind a power box holding the local electricity supply. A flock of Angels passed, and in this moment of relief I climbed atop it, to hoist myself onto the low rooftop. The sound of the returning patrol produced enough adrenaline in me to pull myself up, arms weakened by malnourishment, through a shattered window. I fell through into a dusty bathroom, shards of glass sticking into my coat, and crawled into the tub that lay by the far wall. I tried to silence my breath, but the panicked chemistry of my body coursed through my nerves and veins with a furious volume, blood deafening. I lay low on my stomach like a hunter watching a stag, whereby a single movement could give my location away. But I, of course, was the hunted.

It turned dark, and as the hours passed, the terror subsided. I drifted over the borders of my unconscious and back, a smuggler of memory into my waking brain. I was able to look directly, for the first time, at the trauma of Judgement Day. Until then I had only glimpsed it around the edges of my perception, as flashes of searing light that hit like a headache whose debilitation was to be avoided. Then, I would place a cool flannel on my forehead or succumb to a short lie-down in the dark, for the physical and psychological after-effects of that calamity threatened the completion of my daily tasks. Lying in that freezing bath, I faced the images that resurfaced.

The massacres seemed unnecessarily bloody. On that day on the hills and through those that followed it had become clear that punishment itself was a thrill to heaven, that He regarded the bodies He gathered as his gift, their misuse in sin as a personal insult, and the pooling of blood as his right. This blood – vibrant, clotted, smeared on the room's walls in desperate handprints – returned to me. Was this the grace of God?

I had stayed after the angelic judgement in the hope that there would be some renewal, that the city would rise as the new Jerusalem. But the map didn't make sense any more. The border no longer lay between the city and the fields, but between heaven and earth. If I fell into the Angels' hands having survived this long, my prior rank would not reserve me some preferential treatment. The present darkness brought clarity to my vision: there was no future for me here. I made my decision to go.

It was deep in the night before I dared to venture out of the bathtub. The wooden floorboards let out a creak as I stood up. I opened the medicine cabinet; inside were the remnants of a quiet domestic life. An expensive brand of toothpaste, the tube half-rolled, and a badger-hair shaving brush and cut-throat razor. I flicked it open – still sharp – and pocketed it as a weapon, if not against an Angel then against any thief I might encounter. I slipped the other items into my coat too; looting had become a necessary habit. Ibuprofen, talcum powder, indigestion tablets, calamine lotion, and cough syrup, whose weight and presence – that of a slim whisky bottle – in my inside pocket gave me reassurance. I edged the bathroom door open and peered out.

The home looked like it had been well loved. On the patterned wallpaper black-and-white photographs of children hung crooked in the aftermath of the blasts that must have swept through the house. I crept up the stairs to see if there was anything else worth pilfering, but the floorboards of the landing had fallen through, and the doors were off their hinges. I peered over the chasm into the room below. It was impeccable, with no sign, as far as I could tell, of either a forced entry or a chaotic exit. Maybe the family who had lived here were good, genuinely good. Maybe they were one of the few to have been raptured. I made my way back down, clicked open the lock, and slipped out into the night.

I didn't go back to my apartment. I didn't trust my neighbour, for one thing. She may have been a good citizen but she would shop me just as readily as she had fed me all sorts of information about our other neighbours. No, the longer I deliberated the sooner they'd notice I was gone. I headed straight for the street of boarded-up shops, and to a bodega that had been there for decades longer than I had been alive. The metal shutters had been peeled back from the bottom like a sardine tin, just enough for me to squeeze through. Glass shards covered the floor; it was no surprise that the store had already been looted for its crates of imported champagnes and shelves of aged brandies.

Once a neighbourhood hub of trade, gossip and argument, it might have been closed for centuries, so absent of life was it now. I had come here because it was local knowledge that it had also been a den of iniquity, where in the back, bets and wagers were won and lost, cards and dice thrown, and knives drawn. Using my hands as guides in the dark, I felt my way down a short corridor into the back room. The place was in disarray, tables and chairs overturned. On the nearside wall, the flag of the city still hung, untorn. I had not seen these omnipresent silks since the flames; how fragile such a flag now seemed, where before it flew for immutable power. I ran the back of my hand across its smooth surface.

On the back wall stood a hefty cupboard on which were piled cut-glass carafes and tankards. My eyes adjusting to the unlit room, I paced around looking for something to break open its locked and bolted doors. In the corner were three steel bars, used to jemmy the huge barrels supplied to bars and restaurants into the front of the shop. I took one and tried to force the lock, but I didn't have the patience or the knack, and instead swung it straight at the wood panels, which shattered with splinters crossing the room.

The cupboard was bare, and I reached right in, to the back where I knew I could find a little cut in the board. I pulled it; it scarcely gave. But another tug and the board started to shuffle forward, until the whole thing came out. I tossed it aside. There, I could make out a tunnel, wide enough for someone to push a barrel through. I had seen it being used when I was a teenager, when my father brought me to the bodega when his shipment arrived. He played cards with Alfonso, the late store owner and grandson of the founder. A minor infractor of the law, who meant no harm but never paid full price for anything.

The tunnel looked to open up after a few metres, then dipped down steeply. Water pooled on the floor, soaking my clothes as I burrowed down. Abandoning my city like this felt unfaithful, but what else could I do? I had become so poor in wealth, body and spirit as to buy into the myth of the Tafurs, to believe in that place beyond.

Thresholds are hardest to cross when they mark a transfer from one authority to another, from one sense of existence to another. The Roman Republic was held together in a testy peace by the export of violence. Those men we learned of in school history, *gladii* gleaming in their hands, they carried off their conquests to lands beyond the Roman provinces. Yet within the limits of the republic, marked by the banks of the Rubicon River, their rule was illegal. No governor could march his legions over the river without risking death. It was Caesar who crossed it, and Caesar who won. I felt the danger of passing from the authority of the Holy Occupation to the anarchy beyond the walls, and then, if I made it, to the Tafurs – but still I crossed.

The crossing was physically hard – to hunt down the smugglers' route and find the courage to crawl through under the cover of failing light. Harder to bear, though, was traversing between one world and another, from one law to another. To admit one has already begun one's pilgrimage.

Under the former regime, pre-occupation, my everyday had been a ticking metronome set to beat a set of iron rules. There were people who I had to consult and stamps I had to attain in order to perform my professional actions, and there were others who sought out my help, and between the two only a thumb-wide gap, a postage stamp of discretion, in which I could perform my life and make my mark. The destruction of the occupation delivered untold fear upon us, but I was still a citizen, residing in my city. Now that I had escaped, the one unchangeable thing, which had endured through everything – my citizenship – was gone. The citizen I had been was buried in the earth beneath those walls.

As I grabbed for a branch to pull myself up out of the tunnel, I realised I was in a place of no such rule. From now on, I thought, I cannot be powerful, so I shall have to be wise.

A muddy pigsty was my rude welcome to the other side. I found my way to a thicket, and looked up through the branches. Far from the smog of the city, the sky was as clear as a well. The brightest star I'd ever seen glowed above. I'd reached a no-place in which I was answerable only to myself.

I had no specific place in mind to head to, but I knew from my previous work just how you gain control of a territory. It was clear the ferocity of the initial invasion was intended to be total; its prolongation cast doubt on its divine justice. Still, it had overwhelmed any hope of organised resistance. The city was under their control. They could be rolling out across this land soon, the Angels, the flames, the courts upon His right and left hand. I approached the agricultural hinterlands in the hope that I could find a group to join, and for which to offer my help. To begin with, the idea that I might come across my comrades from the administration guided my movements. I was on the lookout for organisers, for alternatives. In vain.

As soon as I was out in the hinterland I felt my body changing. I was getting fitter, with all the walking. How many miles I tread in those first few weeks, desperate to put the column of smoke that covered the city behind me. My sedentary lifestyle, bound in all ways to my desk, had made me soft, unused to the physical wear of fugitive movement. No matter, I pushed on, my mouth wordless in the first flush of this itinerant life. I trudged along with my head down and would have cut a tragic figure against the landscape to any onlookers. Weight dropped from my already light frame as my only food was foraged or found – roots and berries and the like. I made escapades into abandoned farmhouses where I could pick up some aged cheese, unchilled cans of coke from reeking refrigerators, or domestic items. In one I found a knapsack on the porch, and a heavy-bottomed saucepan in the open kitchen, which I packed into it. In another, a canteen light enough to stow.

By the time my first blisters had worn into calluses, I was an adept at rough living, yet some things I couldn't prepare for. You woke up alone and you would go to sleep alone, and in between there was no one but yourself for company. Previously defined by the diaries of city life, I now had to get to know myself not in relation to charts and computer programmes, but to the happenstance of each day's experience. This, I supposed, was the experience of a refugee. It took me a while to realise that this is what I had become – stateless. No longer a person with a neighbourhood, a history, a file of accomplishments and a to-do list for the coming year; no longer an established subject within a network of contacts, but a displaced person, understood in the terms and situation of the present, in the list of challenges I faced between now and the next satiation of my needs.

I followed the lower contours of the foothills that flanked the west of the city, along the edge of the valley, which rose away from the desolation that had been visited upon us. Eventually the tower of smoke disappeared beyond the horizon, and the wind caught a fresh chill. Ahead of me lay a bluff, rugged and treeless, stripped bare from generations of grazing. It took me four days to climb in all, as I headed for a cut in the mountain range where a pass stretched between this valley and the next. I felt exposed; heavenly lights still played on me daily, and while the city was no longer visible, the breaking clouds that threw down a Jacob's Ladder of justice could still be seen far away. I was never out of sight, I thought, even if I was currently unnoticed. The atmosphere was freezing as the altitude increased. I felt it against my skin, inside my lungs, and in my very isolation. The days blended together, just the morning dew drying in the crystal light of the sun, and the occasional stream to cross and drink from. It took its toll on me, mentally surfacing at night; I wondered for how long I would remain within this featureless life, shrinking from the cold, without destination, but climbing higher.

In this humbling landscape, something was growing within me: the realisation that there exists for each of us a place of grace. I had had no tongue to talk of this blessed state before, only morality and cleanliness. I had never experienced this grace, not in my daily life before the end, and not in the behaviour of God and His Angels in the conflagration. Beneath the Angels I knew I had light. Judgement Day is not so different from any other day, at least in its vision of the world needing to be purified for a great revelation. I left my urban home looking less for revelation than for a change in state. Leaving behind the city of disgrace, I

Was not searching for a new law written in the same hand, but for an unknown language through which we could consider grace.

At the top of the range, I did something I had never done before. I performed an expiation for the life I was leaving behind. First, the old law, crossed under the city walls; second, the old self, crossed over on this mountain path at the setting of the sun. My worn body dragged my soul over the threshold with little hope of relief on the other side. I expected more burning cities across the plain. I sat with my anxiety, my regret. I didn't dwell too deeply on what I could have done differently, what I would do again. Here in this moment, between past and future, I could only accept that the violence I had done was wrong, and that my acknowledgement of this could play no role now in its undoing.

When I crossed over the precipice my luck turned. Exhausted, the night hard on the heels of the evening, I allowed my feet to carry me. My head was lost not even in its own thoughts, just floating. The first wisps of the fatty smoke I breathed in didn't register as much more than a pleasant memory. I lingered on the notes of the scent – it was unmistakably meaty, juicy flesh and braising fat and the smoke of oak, perhaps. It seemed to be coming through the wooded thicket alongside the gurgling brook that ran between here and there. I looked hard into the dark, but could see nothing. I turned my head and cupped my ear, but the last birds, the stream, the whispering trees conspired against me. The smell departed, by which time I had recognised it as a sure sign of cultured life: cooking.

I had to fight my way into the forest. A brutal barbed wire of brambles surrounded it. I tried to press them down with my sleeve wrapped in the shawl I used for sleeping in, and eventually broke through into the wood behind. It was like a holy cloister cloaked in mourning cloth. The firm but slender trunks of the coniferous trees rose tall before breaking out into a canopy. All light from the clustered galaxies above was covered by the treetops; only occasionally would a shaft from the moon illuminate the labyrinth. I had to follow my nose, and this led to a core feeling of unease. Although I knew there must be people inside this forest, I had not seen another human in more than a month. The sensation was clear: my dark predator was more likely of supernatural origin.

I jumped at the first murmurs – I'd worked myself up into such a state that the crackle of the forest floor and whistle of the branches were obscured by my breathing. The noise that broke through was harsh, so crude to my ears that it took a moment to place it as a man's laughter. I turned to my right, where a break in the trees a little further on revealed the moon, and I saw the wisps of smoke passing through the clearing. What a thrill to remember good humour! It rekindled a sense of looking forward to something. Ahead of me was a basic shelter, camouflaged on the sloping side with moss and leaves. As I approached, I rehearsed in my head a few lines, imagining the stunned faces around the fire, and wondered who it was I should introduce to them.

VII

WHAT HUMANITY did we have, those of us whom circumstances had forced into living as beasts in the woods? There was no warm welcome from the group. They grunted at me on my approach, without question or contestation. They were absorbed in eating from a communal pot, and I couldn't read either hospitality or defensiveness on their faces. After devouring their food, they slept where they lay, higgledy-piggledy across bodies, without seemingly any emotional connection. There were no caresses or tongues running along tongues; there was no desire among their overlapping limbs. They must have come from the city, judging by what marks and tassels I could make out on their clothes. I found it fascinating that they had descended into such a bestial life – their bedraggled state and vulgar behaviours around food and excretion, and the manner in which they treated each other, men, women and children alike. There was no sympathy or love in this crude camp, no charity or care. No value attributed to one or the other, and no concern paid. Neither was there cruelty for cruelty's sake. It seemed they had forgotten what the city had raised in them.

I found myself most shocked by how they all communicated with snarling teeth and base grunts. Without words, what hope did this pitiful band have at coming into a relationship with themselves? The first people I had come across since leaving the walls, their behaviours betrayed souls so harmed that there was no way I could be taken into this mass. I alienated myself, and watched their rituals from a distance. Out of habit, I began to divide them up according to my categories from the administration: clean or unclean, sick or healthy, the efficient and hardworking from the slovenly and incapable. If I had those powers here, I thought, I could lick them into a more comprehensible shape. None were good, but some were clearly useful. I was an outsider too, my superior abilities were useless here, and so I retreated to that first position of control: observation.

I squatted among them for a couple of days, trying to allow my grazed legs, which would not carry me much further, the chance to recover. I had nothing in common with these people, and they offered little nurture beyond a share of the crock-pot. I did not trust the men. There was a young woman whose eyes betrayed a human sentiment that I did not perceive in the others, a glint of panic behind her outward aggression. Her hair was cropped short on one side, and her forearms showed several tattoos. How sharply they stood out in this environment, these drawings that had to be deciphered in relation to the city.

I followed her, at a distance, to the nearby stream that cut through the trees one morning. She was only slightly younger than me, but she held herself apart, with a pugnacity I felt could work in my favour if she were on my side. She rolled up her sleeves and dipped her arms down to the elbow in the water, her skin tight and soft on the inner side. Behind the tree I shivered. I crouched down close to the ground and she looked up at me, narrowing her eyes.

I made myself smaller, to minimise the threat. As she continued to wash one hand with the other, I mimicked the action in the dry dirt, nodding at her. Her body untensed. Her eyes cast down to her washing action, damp, and back up to mine, dry. I wanted to ask if I could join her, but all that emerged from my throat was the same guttural sound as the brutes' back at camp. No words formed, but a grunt, and she responded with a long sigh, as if she were pushing all the air out of her lungs. It gave cautious solace to me and I nodded once more. I scuttled across the forest floor towards her and she rocked back on her haunches. She let out another noise, from the jaw. 'Heerrrr' was the closest approximation, and I echoed it back. She smiled to herself as she let water drain from her palms, as if reminded of a joke. The water splashed and ran down her decorated forearms. So strange, I thought, to see these symbols of a plastic culture, a civilisation of abstraction and form, deep in the forest. In the city, the punk before me would have signified something primitive, someone who had come from nature and never returned. Here, she stood for artifice, something that could turn the whole earth into a fetish. The wild girl was the most visibly urban, and although I would have placed an order on her back within the city walls, here I loved her for it. I watched her run her fingers up her arms, and she snapped at me: 'What, honey?'

'What fuck,' I bit.

'Noffin.'

She laughed at me, poked her tongue out, and held it in her curled fingers. I laughed too, and stuck my tongue right out, for the first time since I was a girl.

I hadn't chosen my single life in the city myself. It's a sin, I believe, to lead your child without their consent into a life of austere bureaucracy. The administration I worked for was, theoretically, militaristic in its organisation, the most violent arm of state enforcement short of the City Guards. Relationships were forbidden, although leaving the service upon marriage was common, a rite of passage in fact. Those who worked there until retirement became curious officials, having renounced conventional relationships. But there was sex, among us and between us and civilians, outliers, prisoners and charges. How am I supposed to justify it? I do not: it was a charged workplace where you had to punish yourself to avoid sin. Perhaps we had to be the state-approved sinners in order to keep the rest of the city clean. Redemption as taught in the churches always entailed violence before cleansing. In any case, I still find the entanglements of sexual power hard to navigate; to understand that what made me desirable was the redemption my discretion afforded. For many, there was something captivating about my position, and I include myself in that number. What I mean to say is: I too am a miserable sinner as is everyone in any uniform and I was sorry for that then and sorry for it when I stared at her washing her forearms.

I was shocked at my language, I had always prided myself on being thoughtful and articulate. Yet here I was, hooting some lost words at her, trying to refind a language that must have been cut out of me at some point. Perhaps the girl was the same as me; a lyricist in urban life who here became another pig. Did she then think of me as I did of her? The way she cut her eyes in my direction, listless and shifty, which I had taken for cunning – could it not just as well have been a curious suspicion?

It hadn't escaped my thoughts since leaving that many of those who had managed to flee were not actually the rich, but rather the smart. Those who had kept the city moving by running an essential black market; those who knew trade at its freest. The occupation had made me a criminal and thief in aid of survival, so those who were already criminals and thieves must have been at an advantage. Whereas for people like me, to escape meant a further shift in mode, for them it was just another backdrop. The wiliest would have put their skills to use in finding exile, the way the guilty and corrupt always emigrate upon a change in regime. This band was probably full of former bootleggers and blacklegs – and here I was among them.

The likelihood was low, but each night as I tried to tuck myself in at the edge of the hut, I wondered whether any of these brutish people recognised me. Perhaps they already had, and were making plans to attack me while I slept; maybe I wouldn't wake until the strike of a sharp-edged boulder ploughed into my dreaming forehead, splitting open my thoughts to the dark sky. As I slipped in and out of consciousness each night, I replayed the images of the last days – the bloody beasts, the carnage, the radiant boy, the naked woman, the citizens' hopelessness. Sometimes I would wake to the muffled sound of others weeping too; a shared camp of salty tears bit back against the cold air.

The girl stopped washing herself and stayed squatted on the riverbank. I kneeled on the opposite side. Looking closely at her face as she scrunched her features at me, I could tell that my department had encountered her before. There was no way a whore like this, young and inked, rough-fighting down to her fingernails, could have escaped our attention. The City Guards would have hauled her before us count-less times, and we would have snatched her into one of the clinics in an instant. Her encounters with our hygienic regime must have toughened her to the point that she could survive such divine apocalypse.

Yet here we were levelled by roughness. She cupped her palms back into the water, raising a handful to my face. 'Bath,' she instructed, and I dipped my hands in, using one to wash the other, my arms, my face. I washed my feet, which had been scored and scratched by the forest floor, and the raw flesh smarted. She began to wash hers too; we sat there facing each other, quietly performing these ablutions. Her heel had an infected blister that was pustulating into an abscess; it needed to be treated and washed out, before it spread and overwhelmed her system. No wonder her eyes looked so bloodshot, I thought, her immune system must be worn out. I reached for her ankle and she shrunk back in panic from my touch, so I reached again, more gently.

She let me bathe the foot, taking care not to poke the abscess. Then I washed a small thorn from a bush, and gripped it between two fingers. I looked into her eyes, then plunged the thorn into her swollen heel. Her wail echoed around the forest and she bucked as though tasered, but I held her ankle fast between my body and arm. Her fingers dug into the earth as I pushed around the edges of the bubo with my thumb, and a yellow-green pus seeped in rivulets down into the clear river water. I dipped her whole foot into the icy stream, and she whimpered as we observed the remains of creamy ill humours carried away with the current. Her foot turned white from the cold, and I removed it from the water, as clean as it ever would be, and elevated her leg on a fallen branch to prevent further bleeding. At last, she smiled.

As I withdrew the thorn from the foot of the girl, I thought back to a story I had first heard as a child, St Jerome and the Lion. Living his ascetic life in the wilderness, St Jerome encounters a raving lion, frothing at the mouth. Rather than kill the beast, as we are led to believe most men would do, Jerome looks for the cause of his rage. A thorn has gotten stuck in its wide, defenceless paw. Jerome, in his beneficence, removes the thorn, thus placating the lion, and earning his trust.

What fear men have of lions! What terror their roar holds! The lion is a creature magnified in the minds of men. They are jealous of the lion – of his power, the enclosed nature of his family, and the offerings of members of his harem, dignified and multiple. The lion is the ultimate prey, a force that never surrenders and so can only be overcome. Men hope in vain that smearing lion's blood on themselves will bestow them with the creature's attributes, as if humility and honour could permeate the skin. But virtues cannot be hunted. Such an act of covetousness would make the skin as impenetrable as leather, so that nothing could pass into the body, which in any case holds emotional forms in its humours.

Still man resists the lion's call from the wilderness. He fears what message he brings from beyond the walls of the city, what terrifying truths he might learn from lands unconquered. Severus Ibn al-Muqaffa', ساويرس بن المقفع, said that Mark the Evangelist finds form in the avatar of a winged lion because, when in the desert with his father they were accosted by a lion and a lioness, Mark prayed to Jesus for redemption and God delivered the pair from the creatures by slaying them before his eyes. I find it hard to believe. That Mark, who was already full of courage, would fear the lions seems preposterous to me. There is nothing the lions could bring to Mark that he did not know or that could destroy him. Mark wrote in his gospel of that first lion, St John the Baptist, who was sent before Christ to prepare the way. John, said Mark, had the *voice of one crying in the wilderness*, to make straight the paths. I had thought often of John on my journey from the city; he baptised in the wilderness, where people found their straighter path. When I found this tribe, and when we sat around the fire, I thought of John, and his feast whereupon I had my first vision.

How many of his wild feast days had I experienced in my life? The feast's eve came around the time of summer solstice. In the day of the eve we would venture out of the city walls up into the hills and pick the herbs that were to fill our medicine cabinets for the coming year: rosemary, lemon verbena, laburnum, foxglove, fennel and rue, and especially St John's wort. We would fill a bucket by the doors of our apartments with water and leave the herbs inside to stew, and upon his feast, we could wash our faces with them, the water cleaning off the dirt that had accumulated. This way, health was acquired. As a child it was my first lesson in the importance of both physical and spiritual hygiene, the beginning of an obsession that would shape my life.

The city was crazed with explosions, riotous burning, and firecrackers thrown in the street. Oh, and the fires, the fires . . . In every square, without concern for life or property, monumental bonfires of dry wood and bones would lick the night sky. People would gather with friends, strolling from fire to fire, and drink sweetened wine, and sing, and light fireworks that would shoot up above the pall, exploding like flowers in the darkness. The noise would wake the dead. As the Evangelist St John wrote, *He was not that Light, but was sent to bear witness of that Light. That was the true Light, which lighteth every man that cometh into the world.*

And from that mass, the nights would indeed draw in, the darkness growing, for *He must increase, but I must decrease*, until they were at their longest in midwinter, when Christ the Light would return. I did not know then, in a city that was lit all hours of day and night, what meaning that light, that fire, would come to have. With the occupation, fire arrived with intensity but light was extinguished. Later, in total darkness, I would refind the light, after the twisting roads of exile had been made straight.

Sitting by the brook, I couldn't help but think of myself in the light of St Jerome, with the girl in the place of the lion. As I bound her foot with a rag, I wondered what tender truths her presence might bring. Now calm, she cleared her throat.

'Doctor,' she uttered, ennobling me with her gratitude. Then she ran her fingers through my long hair.

I had made my first friend outside the city, my first friend in exile, and – I couldn't help but notice – through the application of hygiene. It helps, I thought, it helps.

We arrived back at the camp together, but nobody noticed.

The next day, I joined a gang who headed from the forest down the hillside towards the fortified farms to snatch eggs from chicken coops and tear up potatoes from abandoned fields. That night, having cooked the food and shared it among us, I fell into a half-doze by the girl, who nestled her head against me. I was exhausted, and stuffed with food, which was what kept me in the camp, enabling me to put some flesh back on my bag of bones, returning some health to my stomach.

The sustenance returning to me gave me the chance to think past my immediate survival. I escaped the city to put distance between my self and my sin, between myself and unfolding punishment. Was that punishment following me out into the wilds? Within the forest we found ourselves wretched but sustained, both physically and morally speaking. Above us grew the canopy through which we found our dappled light, while the land, harvested as a group, provided us with ample food. We were grateful for this place, for this greenness. For the creatures of the forest, for the mushroom and fungi, for the mulching leaves and the fresh shoots. Among nature's growth, there was the will to go on. As sleep encroached on the encampment, I looked up at the canopy, the fire illuminating its frondescence in the night. Beneath our weary bodies the same trees held together our earth. I was moved by what I also feared – the unremitting refusal of nature to stop being.

Moving away from the city, I sensed within nature a rhythm beyond human control. I was merely another node in its network, in its infinite expansion. This holy movement of life, which overwhelms the limits of language, I have come to call *viriditas*. This term is merely a gesture towards all which is sacred, uncapturable. Only God, the true divinity that lives in all of the vibrating atoms of the universe can unite the substance and the sign.

The stars broke through the trees, and I counted off the constellations as they cradled our sleep. My eyes focused in the direction of Polaris. My heart ached to see it. I must continue this journey, I thought, further away from the city. I felt the calling towards flight. I knew not what the purpose of this passage, the movement of blood around the body, since the visions of the first days was, simply that this had become a pilgrimage. I could not imagine what lay before me, but I was no longer burdened by the shame of exile. My past home was in flames, so it was only through a kindling of the fire within me that I could reach my next destination.

The pole star marks the tip of the Ursa Minor constellation, the little bear. I made a prayer to St Ursula, and thought of her fated journey. Filled with hope for her advancing nuptials, she was crossing a continent accompanied by eleven thousand fellow virgins when they were trapped inside the walls of a city by a horde not unlike my terrorisers, godless and cruel. They shot her with an arrow and beheaded the eleven thousand, their blood a bath contained by the walls, staining the battlements. I imagined her last moments. Ursula, the brave bear, ahead of eleven thousand virgins, and me, lying in the dirt with this flirtatious whore, my hands running through her hair as she slept. I wondered whether my martyrdom lay somewhere inside the girl, inside the envelope of her skin. If a pilgrimage to meet her body and soul might grace me with another divine experience . . . Didn't Jesus find redemption in the arms of a whore, too? Were not bodies our own vehicles for worship? She moved her body in line with mine, hip connecting to hip, arm with arm, breast with breast, equals beneath our blanket. As Ursula gave up her marital bed for her holy blood, I considered what I might sacrifice for purification and redemption.

I felt the presence of ghosts all around me that night, as I lay awake in her warmth. I considered the victims of my clinic, those who were kept awake at the thought of my industrious staff. Those women were sacrificial vessels, not one of them a virgin, not innocent but far from guilty. The girl pushed her backside into the nook of my front body. I would have willingly done it, I knew it then, as I held her hips in my hands. She offered herself to me, and I took her as willingly as I would have taken them. I dipped my head forward, my lips touching the back of her neck for the first time. At the back of my throat reverberated a song I used to hum as I removed my surgical gloves and scrubbed my hands in hot soapy water.

When the voice of Ursula's blood,
and of the blood of her innocent host,
sounded before God's throne,
an ancient prophecy passed
through the root of Mamre and spoke
in the revealed truth
of the Trinity:
'This blood touches us;
let us all now rejoice!'

And afterwards the congregation of the Lamb came,
through the ram caught in the thorns,
and said:
'Let there be praise in Jerusalem

This stands for priests
who disclose God with their mouths

and cannot see him in full.
And they said: 'O noblest host:
that Virgin called Ursula on earth
is named Columba (Dove) in heaven,
because she gathered around her a host
of innocents.'

O Ecclesia: you are worthy of praise
in that host.

That great host which is signified
by the unconsumed bush Moses saw,
and which God planted in the first root
in the human being he made of earth,
so that it might have life without any
mixture with man:
that host called out in a radiant voice
in purest gold, topaz, sapphire,
all set in gold.

Now let all the heavens rejoice,
and let all peoples be honoured with them.
Amen.

Our gang of gleaners could only offer so much. The valley in which we were now camping was running short on supplies from the former farmland, and there was enough left for a week or two at most. At night the sky saw flashes of light coming from over the horizon, and deep rumblings from the earth portended that the occupation had surpassed the sinful city and was rolling out across the wider territory. The group began to split. Some began gathering more than just food, stripping whatever they could during the raids. Carts were pilfered from barns, telephone and fiber-optic cables rolled into thick spools, fuel decanted from tanks in yards.

During one raid, the girl and I broke into the main building of a farmhouse, leaving the rest of the party to carry back sacks of potatoes while we ransacked the house in secret. In the kitchen, I found a drawer of silver cutlery, which I tied together with linen tea towels and stashed in my waistband. Upstairs, she was rifling through the bedrooms looking for jewellery and gold. After I'd finished with the living quarters and outbuildings, I went up to find her. The door to the master bedroom was open, drawers pulled out of every bedside table and cabinet, their contents of painkillers, reading glasses, letters and tea lights scattered on the floor.

I could hear the sound of running water. At the far end of the room the door to the en-suite was ajar.

I pushed it wider to catch her unravelling the piece of purple cloth she'd fashioned into a cummerbund, her form set off against the lavender-painted walls. On the floor a piece of calico was laid with a host of jewels, rings, necklaces and precious stones. I guessed she felt my presence, but pretending not to, she lifted her hair up before shaking it out. I could smell her from across the room – mould and wood smoke – over the scent of the bath salts. She must have managed to light the boiler for the luxury of a hot bath. Like her arms, her back and legs were covered in tattoos. She turned to face me, unabashed. 'Bath,' she uttered with a smile, and climbed in.

I pulled up a straw stool and sat down next to the bath, over her jewels. I picked them up individually and held them up to the skylight. One by one, I dipped them in her bathwater as she washed, then wiped them dry on my skirt. Some were uncut, most were carved to fit their cases, and the largest was a green gemstone, smooth and uncorrupted. 'Green,' she said.

'Smaragdus. Emruld,' I replied. I wanted to share their true wealth with her; beyond their material beauty, their curative properties, induced by God, saved from loss when Lucifer tumbled from heaven. I laid them out on the calico in a circle.

The wind was picking up around the farmhouse, bringing with it the darkness. It would have been wise to get back to the camp, following our tracks, but neither of us suggested this. With the wind might come rain, washing away our footprints. Or worse, the gusts might bring the next stages of the occupation. God knows it was close, and getting closer. We all knew we had dwelled too long in this valley, feasted too much on the juicy oranges that had swelled the orchards. Staying here in the farmhouse was foolish – the girl knew it too – but for the first time since I had begun this fool's progress, I found myself motivated by a need higher than base survival.

There wasn't a force in the world that could take me away from this primitive companionship, and that night I simply chose not to return. I wanted to stay with her, watching her wash. I returned downstairs for my knapsack, and brought it back to the steaming bathroom. I pulled out a leather pouch in which was stored a zip-lock bag from the city, and inside this, a few plastic cigarette lighters. On top of a chest by the far wall was a copper tray of candles, which I lit one by one, and distributed around the room. I took a towel from inside the chest and pressed it against my cheek: a moment of urban comfort, a retreat back to business trips that took me to hotels. The first drops of rain rapped against the exposed rafters. But the room was insulated tight against the elements. The other abodes we'd stormed hadn't been so untouched; they'd already been stripped, either by their inhabitants upon leaving, by locals before us, or by other savage bands. But in the heart of this house was this pristine chamber.

The girl continued bathing, rubbing the washcloth around her neck before submerging herself in the white suds, fast becoming brownish with her filth. On the lavatory cistern I noticed a slim book of recipes, and flicked through it in remembrance of the city's cornucopia: game pies, jugged hare; steamed broad beans tossed in olive oil, lemon juice and mint; whole roasted artichokes with thyme. I felt my stomach roar with the memory.

I returned to my seat and dug into the bag of food I had filled downstairs. There was a round of spelt bread (stale, but its nutritional goodness covered a multitude of upsets and sicknesses), two pomegranates, and a piece of ripe cheese, oozing inside its paper wrapping. I broke off a crust of the loaf, dipped it into the cheese, and handed it to the girl. She hadn't expected the first serving, and grinned as she took it. I took my serving. In the flickering light, we felt the soothing fat of the cheese sticking to the inside of our mouths. Her mouth was still full when she formed the first whole sentence I'd heard from her: 'This cheese is absolutely delicious.'

The room had warmed considerably and I pulled off the padded leather that I had worn almost the whole time since leaving. My arms were at last unrestrained, my shoulders agile. I pulled my hair loose and took off my boots. She breathed in the room's close atmosphere, the shared sense of bodily care.

The pomegranate split beneath my fingernails and spilled its rich juice across the copper tray and down my forearms. I sucked at the fruit to try to quell the juices. The first wet rush abated, I left one half on the tray, and used my thumbs to push the skin of the other until it inverted, the segments of jewel-like seeds standing proudly. Using the back of my hand, I beat the fruit so that the seeds rained down onto the tray into a pool of their blood. I balanced the tray on the edge of the bath, and we picked at the fruit together, holding a pinch of seeds above our open mouths and dropping them in as if we were Roman wives. The girl missed, and a streak of red left her lips and trickled down the side of her cheek, its final drop falling with the seed into the bathwater. She giggled, and I giggled, and she giggled more, and before I could help it we were laughing like schoolgirls as she sank into the bath and tried to catch the seed like an alligator between her teeth. Her laughter made her blow bubbles and the mirth carried between us, almost innocents in this passing shelter from the blustering storm.

Pomegranate finished, the girl got out of the bath. I was folding the gems back into their calico wrapping when she began to refill the tub.

'What for?' I asked her.

'You take the bath,' she replied.

I tried to remonstrate with her: it was time for us to leave. If we stayed there any longer the worsening storm would make it impossible for us to reach the camp in the dark.

'It's too late.'

I knew, and now wondered why I hadn't implored her to leave earlier. It was already too dangerous to risk our transit through the fields and the woods, full as they were with boars and wolves and men. 'No, no bath,' I insisted, but she ignored me, running her hand back and forth through the rippling water. It had been years since I had taken a real bath. I permitted myself.

My clothes were disgusting to remove; hair seemed to have grown into the seams, and they were almost sticky to touch. Beside her new cleanliness, I felt like a beastly berserker, but she helped to unlace me despite my protestations. Soon I was naked before her. She did not avert her eyes; unlike me, she did not shy away from bare flesh. While my embarrassment represented itself in a scarlet blush across my chest, for her, my skin was me and I was my skin. I stepped unsteadily into the bath and she seated herself on my peasant's throne. Up close I studied the tattoo drawn across her chest in cheap ink: a horned horse, not flying across the heavens like Pegasus but grazing on a pasture. I stared at the horse, and at her lovely face, and thought of the holy unicorn hunt with a novel sympathy towards the animal, who I knew to be so easily beguiled by a young woman's beauty.

I sank blissfully into the intense heat of the water. I felt it draw my blood to the surface of my skin, flushing it as pink as my blush. It acted as a soporific balm for this bruised and aching body. As my corpse relaxed I let my mind become engulfed; I let go.

Through the steam I could see her rubbing herself with one of the plush towels, wrapping another deftly around her hair. First an arm appeared to steady her body against the edge of the bath, slender and purposeful. The arm retreated into the opaque cloud and I drifted out of consciousness. Inside the white cloud a spark of fire, ignited and reignited, produced the unmistakable scent of clove, cinnamon and tobacco as she dragged on her hand-rolled cigarette. She was traceable within the fog only by her light. I let it seduce me into a searing sleep, my head rolling back against the enamel.

In my dream, I was in a clinical white-tiled room, attended by a team of smocked women who were preparing my body for burial. I was lying on a marble fish counter, and the chief mortician sharpened her long filleting knife. Two pulled back the violet velvet shroud that covered my naked body, while another dipped rosemary into a jug of lemon water. The others around me were chatting away, rude gossips whose thirst for news disrupted the solemnity of the occasion.

Upon awakening, the girl was sitting on the edge of the bath. I could only make out her closest edges; not her head, dipped down, nor her arms, reaching to touch something on her lap. She lifted something to breast height, and the musculature of her shoulders and upper back pulsed as she applied a firm pressure. The room reverberated with a violent crack. The back of her head appeared through the mist as she turned and held out her hand.

'Nut?' she asked, and I took half a walnut kernel from her hand. She took the other half and placed it deliberately on the centre of her tongue, showing off its wrinkled form in the soft wetness of her mouth. She closed her mouth and chewed with half a smile, before dropping the shell to the floor. I chewed too. The slightly bitter taste lingered. The heat was becoming so intense I felt delirious. Each of my veins and arteries were raised like causeways, and a black, bilious shame coursed through me in response to the vision of the dark walnut on her pink tongue. I wanted to draw the bile seeping from my organs out of my body and into the water. I no longer wished to be my own captain, but here in the wet wilds outside the walls, there was no one I could depend on to take the ship's wheel. I let myself drift further . . .

Two hands emerged from the cloud, one holding a washcloth that it dipped in the bathwater. My eyes rested above the water, rolling in my motionless head to trace the hands' movement. They wrung out the cloth, and motioned for me to pull myself from the water. As I sat up and hunched forwards like a child, our eyes met. She leaned behind me and began to wash my back, humming a little lullaby. This act was foreign to me, threatening even, and I tensed and closed my eyes in discomfort, while also willing her to never, ever stop. I have performed many deeds of care as charity for many people in my life, but to be the recipient left me feeling powerless.

'Tell me more about stones, sister,' she asked, cupping water in her hands and releasing it down my forehead.

'Precious stones are garnered in the hot rivers of the East,' I began.

'Hot like this bath?'

'Hotter. They are gifts whose earthly powers were crystallised in their beauty when they fell from Lucifer's cape.' She pushed her parted fingers into my hair, dislodging the grease and dirt and foliage that had matted it. 'As they came from heaven, their use can only be for good,' I went on. 'No evil witchcraft is to be conducted with such stones, only good deeds.' The water spilled across my lips, and I could taste burnt wood in it, as if my hair had been seasoned through all the fire. 'I can teach you their meanings, if you'd like?' I offered.

'We have much to learn,' she responded, to which I could find no return.

In the silence, new knowledge vibrated through me, a new language through which my body could speak. Outside, the howling wind met the heartbeat I felt rushing in my ears. A muffled rhythm like inside the womb. My eyes followed her as she rose, still uncovered, and left into the bedroom. Heaving my body from the bath, I shook off my dizziness and dried with the fresh towel she had left for me, wrapped myself, and followed her through. She had lit a fire of dry, crackling twigs in the hearth.

'We will stay,' she said, looking out the low, square window. 'Dangerous to leave now. And no one come tonight, I am sure.'

I sat on the bed, which was properly made, covered with a blanket and over that an embroidered cloth. The detailing was ornate, but by the hand of a single woman. Edged with a border of petunias, the patchwork was composed of a series of panels that together told a story. The first panels showed a farm being worked at harvest time, tractors and hay bales, baskets laden with fruit and sheaves of corn. The next row's panels showed the same men, shouldering firearms and waving farewell, heading out over the mountains. Then there were horses and helicopters, and a long, deep valley like the one we were in, with burning villages. Next came a single panel of a piercing light rendered in metallic threads that seemed to burn. Then there was a tree – a hanging tree, for the butchers to hang their men, but I couldn't focus on it, noticing suddenly my hot nakedness. There were more panels still, but I threw the blanket back, for fear of what tale might come next. Who would be left to embroider the future of the farmhouse upon its marital bed?

'Get in, warm,' the girl said, turning to gesture at me and the bed, although the room was plenty warm already. I slipped beneath the covers and could have slept in an instant, and forever; a sensation so far unfelt in my journey. The room was dark but for the small fire and the flickering chiaroscuro of the candles that she had carried through. I responded to the bed's comfort like one who has struggled with a lengthy task, fighting back fatigue with one arm while pulling themselves forward with the other. On reaching their goal, the body, exhausted, submits to sickness. In this cave of repose with the girl, I felt the debility brought by my losses. My arms fell heavy, weighted beneath the prophetic embroidery she pulled over me. My ribs creaked like a fleet of ancient ships coming into harbour. My anguish found voice in my body while every organ wept in sorrow. Bone touched bone inside my flesh; pain twisted and wrenched my tendons. I sensed a taste on my tongue, the taste of what Jesus must have felt upon the cross, and the suffering produced a glow within me – radiations of pain like when he was pierced by the Lance of Longinus. My wounds opened, the sites of holy depth, welcoming my body to prayer. Lain here in this mortal ruin, I discovered the passage to divine nature, heretofore occluded by urbane morality.

The girl slid in beside me. I was never so aware of

any presence. This was the first time I had ever shared a bed, a real bed, and lying side by side I perceived our every human process: the inhalation of air into our lungs, the blinking of our eyelashes on the pillow, the restlessness of her limbs as they settled into rest. I had the impulse to hold my breath, so as to be able to monitor hers more closely. I wished, and not for the first time, not to be. Not to die, or to be dead, though Lord knows how I walked that path too during those forest nights. A desire not to be; to leave my self to be more within her. If only in that moment, in her proximity, I could dissipate on her breath, melt into a dew on the bedding, be happy. Happier than I had been even before the last days, happy not to be at all.

Is this what they mean by love? To cease being? *She must increase, and I must decrease.*

As I lay with these dissolving thoughts, she turned over with her eyes closed to face me, so each of her breaths landed in my arms. I got the sense, from the pace of her breath, that she wasn't quite asleep. For what felt like an hour, as the dying cinders illuminated the plastered walls, I considered letting my hand fall into hers. The wind outside sounded like it was flagellating the land beyond this haven, the trees battling and bowing to its force. Each gust blew a little more smoke and soot back into the room, adding to the scents.

VIII

*B*ECAUSE THE HUMAN'S SOUL *is from God, it can at times see true and future things while the body is asleep. Then it knows future happenings to the human and sometimes these do occur in this way. It happens often, too, that the soul, exhausted by diabolical delusion or burdened with mental disturbance, cannot see these events clearly and is deceived. For, very often, a human being is also oppressed in his sleep by the thoughts, opinions and aspirations with which he is occupied while awake. And at times – contingent on whether these thoughts are good or evil – he is lifted up in his sleep as yeast lifts up a batch of dough. If the thoughts are good and holy, then often God's grace shows him something true in his sleep. If however the thoughts* *are vain, the Devil sees it and torments the human soul and mixes his own lies into the person's thoughts. The Devil in his mockery shows even disgraceful things about holy people. For when a human while falling asleep is still occupied in his mind with inappropriate joy or sadness, anger or distress, ambition to dominate, or other such things, then the Devil in his derision often holds this up to that person in his sleep because he noticed these things in him while awake. But also, if on some occasion a human falls asleep feeling pleasure of the flesh then, on that occasion, diabolical derision holds this pleasure up to him in such a way that it shows him the bodies of living and, every now and again, the bodies of dead people with whom that person used to be friendly, or even people whom he never saw with his own eyes, so that it appears to him that his is enjoying himself with them in sin and pollution as if he were awake and those who are dead were alive. Thus disgrace befalls his semen.*

I fell into dreaming once again. I passed through the vigilant stage of half-sleep, into my depths. Rarely did I dream before the end, and since then, nearly never. Yet, within the farmhouse's walls, beside the girl, what I had locked in the casket of my body broke out into my sleep.

Whether the thoughts were of the Devil's mockery, I cannot say. Once, I would have known, and would have kept such knowledge to myself, for pollution and contamination spread easily among populations in close quarters to one another. But I cannot tell, so in putting down this dream in full, I endeavour that you might know in turn.

I was destroyed at her feet. I was being dragged by unseen spectres through the corridors of a seedy hotel near the railway terminal. A thousand times I have visited such hells for women, arriving by car and departing by truck. I know their darkness and dampness well, their vanquished bulbs, broken locks and faucets, stench of bodily fluids and chemical lubricants. I was thrown into a room like a criminal into a cell, the air musty with cigar smoke. When I dared to raise my eyes, the girl stood with her back to me, not weak and hobbled by the splinters in her feet, but tall, with her hair pulled tight in a bun behind her head. For the first time in my life I was wearing a mini-skirt that barely covered my backside and she the uniform of an inspector from the Health Administration. In my semi-consciousness I struggled to find my breath, and she smiled a lascivious, self-pleasing smile. My hands were tied behind my back. I was on my knees, head low to the ground, and I could see the rubber boots of the H.A. official before me. I looked up at her: her legs were bound in buckled linen, and a starched white shirt collar protruded out of her short black jacket. In her hand she held a small object, which she used her finger to manipulate around her palm.

My acute distress was tempered by a rising warmth in my head. This was the perverse relief of no longer being in a position of authority in relation to the girl; now that she was promoted to inspector, my duty of care was gone. The room turned cold as I became hot, a sheen of sweat on my skin. The grown girl seemed oblivious to my presence. I tried to get her attention but my voice was breathy, lost to the heat in my head. The harder I tried to draw her to me, the more I desperately wanted her to turn around, but there was no recognition, no awareness of this person in hell at her feet.

From this absurd room the dream shifted. The object in the girl's hands was the walnut she had broken for me that evening. I saw her hands crack the brittle shell again, splitting it into two hemispheres. We crouched over her cupped, closed hands like schoolgirls, and when her palms opened, I saw not a nut but my room in the state seminary.

This room was my adult womb, in which I once gestated alongside my spiritual twin. The room had two doors: one to the corridor of identical cells that

151

ran one hundred metres to the cloisters, and the other to an antechamber in which there was a ceramic toilet and a drain in the centre of the floor for the showerhead mounted on the ceiling. In our cell, everything was doubled and matching. Two iron-framed beds, whose thin mattresses did little to soften the springs below. Two wooden desks at the foot of our beds, where we could study and write in seclusion. Two chests beside the door in which we kept our few possessions – shoes, notepad, linens and the like. The only thing in the singular was the crucifix that hung between our beds.

I shared this room from my enrolment until I began my service in the city, that is, for over ten years. For much of this time, we never left the room, my roommate Jutta and I. We hated it there and for the first month I cried every night, remembering the voice of my grandfather, whom my family had lowered into the ground mere weeks before I was interned. When the nut cracked open, the young girl was there, in her habitual position, lying across her bed, with her stockinged feet pressed up against the cool wall. In that position she would read to me, and we would laugh, the only laughter of my time in the training school, blood rushing to her head as her shoulders heaved.

The cruel life of the seminary was a training in disconnection, in removing the subtle social biases that would hinder us in our vocation, which was a great honour. We were to be the administrative class for our society, entrusted into a position of care, and as such our education was about lifting us from our petty concerns into a regime of devotion towards the city and its citizens. Nobody was without fault, and while Jutta and I were never rebels, we found in each other's company some times of faulty respite. The first years of separation and isolation were soothed only by her presence, her kind words of friendship and feminine wisdom. A few years my elder, she was my first model of womanhood. Jutta, as I dreamed of you. Jutta, your firmness against my indiscretion, your quiet word to my trespass.

The hand closed around the nut, and the girl in the farmhouse held it firm, as if to wish it returned to the whole. We were back in the shared bed, and the memory of our teenage enclosure faded with the blush in my cheeks. The sound of the crozier against our door, the brutality of an education laced with suppression and violence, the coldness I carried with me into my service ... In the presence of the girl, my distant past ceased to be frozen, and sensations swirled in my veins in fluid confusion.

How could she hold the kernel in her hand? How could the one saving grace of my youth, my Jutta, come forth from her palm? She was imbued with the memory of my dear, sweet roommate, from whom I had never heard, nor consciously thought of, since we began our work in the administration.

Outside the storm thundered on, and my body shuddered with fitful dreams. Everything that had settled in my soul was shaken like a snowdome, elevated before falling again. In the midst of dreaming, the wind jolted me awake, to find that the girl had curled up close, clinging to my torso beneath the quilt. Jutta, still with me, steadied my fearful heart with her calm hands once again.

IX

WE WOKE TO DEVASTATION. The storm had scoured the surrounding countryside like a mighty hoe dragged across the earth. I was first to rise. She was still snoozing beside me, and I got out of the bed gently, so as not to wake her. She turned in her sleep, and I covered my body with my hands as I looked for my discarded clothes. Her skin was exposed where I had turned back the blankets; her scars and wounds just looked like more of her tattoos, which were now beautiful to me, and held in my affection as a symbol of our exquisite agony lived together. I wondered when next I would experience a night of such soft temptations.

Downstairs the room was chilly and smelled strongly of smoke. Edging open the front door, the night's carnage was laid out before me. I surveyed the desolate landscape like a soldier in the aftermath of a battle. The bridge that had spanned the river in a gothic arch where the Devil found his souls, that too was washed out. How would we cross back to reach the camp? I sensed her walk up behind me, the smell of clean hair cutting through the sooty air.

'Gone,' she said.

'Aye,' was the most I could respond.

We didn't speak much more. I stirred up a mess of porridge, which we ate straight from the pan with our hands, occasionally picking out the pungent herbs I'd added from between our teeth. She chewed the herbs thoroughly to release their aromas, then spat the fibres in thick gobs onto the floor, grinning. I smiled back, but my heart was full of pain, stuck between night and dawn. I felt a responsibility for this child, and I didn't know if I could deliver on the promises our company had seemed to make the night before. She was my patient, after all, and with only the sack of food gleaned from the farmhouse, and the cracked spine of the bridge for support, my chest weighed heavy. I ignored any gestures she made towards me and busied myself wrapping up what more I could pilfer: a couple of sharp knives, a jar of grains, and the leftover candles and copper tray.

The sun had barely broken across the low hills on the far edge of the valley, but it was time to move on.

'Come, girl,' I said, and she threw the last of her cup of water onto the embers of the fire.

At the gate we stood and stared. The waters beneath the bridge's remains were raging, impossible to cross: our route back was surely severed. Looking up to the hills, it seemed unlikely that the corps of thieves would have survived the night. The pine forest had been flattened – anyone sleeping there that night would have had their camp torn apart. Our time with the crooks and villains was at an end. A return to the city was inconceivable. I wondered whether our bond would be enough to take us further, towards the cut snipped between the tall mountains a hundred or more kilometres away at the end of the valley. We had little choice.

We trekked for days in near silence, stopping rarely. The distant rumbles of divine providence never lessened behind us, and still our destination became no clearer. Presently, I noticed how the countryside around us began to change, as the cultivated land gave way to olive groves and dusty scrub. We had made some distance together.

X

THE ARID GROVES proved a tougher terrain to cross than we had expected. The days were roasting hot but the night's chill brought a persistent dew so that you would wake up damp and shivering. We looked for nooks and ravines to shelter in as the sun began to set. As I was climbing over a low wall, being careful to hold down the rusted barbed wire that ran over it, the girl tapped me on the back. She pointed uphill towards a shepherd's hut, its roof of terracotta tiles and chimney intact. The sun was only just visible above the horizon. Had she pointed out a cave, or a sheepfold, I would have rebuffed her for the sake of a few more kilometres before we set up camp for the night. But the benefits of a solid, dry night's sleep, complete with a slow-burning fire, were exactly what we needed, and would repay us in distance in the following days. We reached the hut before dusk had fully fallen.

We made a happy home for ourselves that night. She swept the floor and lay down our blankets, while I collected what deadwood I could from the field. Inside the hut were the remnants of the shepherd's life: magically, a tin of ground coffee; another of smoked, salted nuts; several books in an indecipherable language; and a crate of ale bottles, all empty but one. I stoked the fire on which to cook our supper of pottage, flavoured with herbs we had foraged during the day and some wild garlic pulled from the riverbank. When it was aromatic and bubbling, I took a bowl out to her, perched on the doorstep, the sun falling across her face. We ate in relative silence, looking out onto the calm valley. It was impossible, in that moment, to perceive any trace of the violence we had witnessed, together or apart. I knew next to nothing of her life before the camp. We did not mention the experience we had shared within the farmhouse, although we did talk back over things we had seen on the journey, before and after. The sexual lasciviousness of the men, and some of the women, who violently divided the den of thieves, creating a cut-throat hierarchy between the bullied and subjugated, and the triumphant and exploitative. We were better off out than in, although life was more challenging, not only because we were away from that communal swamp, but because now we were on a journey.

I cracked the cap of the beer open and poured a little into each of our enamel cups, savouring the first sip. It had been months since I had supped any alcohol and it went straight to my head. The warmth our bodies held from the day's sun was draining away. We retreated inside where the fire had made a toasty fug within the tiny but well-insulated space. Propped up against the rock wall, our bare feet facing the flames, we joked a little and shared our thoughts. As we reached the bottom of the bottle, she asked me what I did, back in the city.

'The city is home?'

'Yes. Most of my life. I work for the city. Worked. Health Administration.' She shivered at the mention. 'I hate H.A.,' she said.

'I know . . .' It was the most I could reassure her. 'I understand.'

I did understand, but I felt a little dishonest, like I was distancing myself, like I had always understood. My short utterance implied at best that I was a do-gooder in the administration, rather than a high-ranking official. Now that the ground had been levelled and a greenness had sprung up between us, I didn't want to risk the confession of my complicity.

'You?' I asked back.

'I survived. Sometimes I worked.' She sipped a little more beer and laughed to herself. 'God. Cigarette. That's good.' A hopeless little prayer, for we had no cigarettes. Her head slumped back against the wall. 'I worked for some time.'

'Doing what?'

'Cheese factory,' she replied. 'Near the citadel.'

She didn't need to tell me; the cheese factory was huge, the result of an attempt to centralise food production almost five decades ago, twice her lifetime, and near enough the only project that had worked. Other subsidiary industries lost out to black market-eering and corruption, and then privatisation. The cheese factory was, as far as I knew, the only central-ised food-processing plant left, and it produced a government-controlled cheese so bland it couldn't attract a single exporter. Once the city was renowned for its cheese culture, churning litres and litres of milk each day according to passed-down family recipes. Then, or until the Judgement, it became a net importer, the richest inhabitants shipping in artisan cheeses from abroad.

'I've not visited,' I said, prompting her to recount her stint in the cheese halls. Hundreds of women worked in each of the three halls, on shifts morning, noon and night. They hand-mixed the contents of the vast vats, which hung like crucibles from metal racks. The environment, she said, was revolting. Dank and reeking of ferment, bleach and rat excrement. (The food hygiene department was separate from mine; we focused on human bodies, they on other, smaller vermin.) The vats were moved along by ex-prisoners, who were also charged with discipline and efficiency monitoring.

'They were rough,' she said, 'with us, as women.' Punishment was physical, and took place in the cheese caves. It was there that she first knew a man, or rather, a group of men. Taken for some minor infraction she wondered whether she might ever see the light of day again. She did, others didn't, she told me, and she left changed.

In the winter, the corrugated iron roof provided no insulation. In their plasticated tabards and worn clogs, the workers' hands would nearly freeze in the whey. In summer, the halls became furnaces, mould was impossible to combat, and they would leave their shifts dehydrated, exhausted and frequently sick.

I had no idea the conditions were so bad. Certainly, everyone knew it wasn't a place you'd ever wish to be sent. But it was honest work, we had assumed, and good for the soul. The picture she painted was a vision of hell.

'That's why you left,' I suggested.

'Take your chances,' she said.

Terrible, such terrible things I must have done at the H.A.

The milk, she explained, came in three types. One thick, almost gelatinous with cream, so thick that you didn't resent when cold splatters landed on your lips. The hall of the thickest dairy was reserved for the well-disciplined, elderly women, who must have reminded the administrators of their kindly mothers. This cheese was rich and accordingly expensive; a festival treat for most citizens, and a cause of gout to the more successful merchants. One thin, that of the central hall, which produced the cheese most of us knew from childhood – mild, going-on flavourless, that melted across your toast or potatoes. The last hall, the girl worked in, at the lowest tier. There, the milk was bad, already on the turn. It was staffed by women caught in crime, and the guards there were the most vicious. This cheese was the cheapest form of fat you could find. Only the poorest citizens could stomach it, but it could make you sick, if you left it out, which, of course, many people did.

The cheese was a punishment for the poor, from start to finish. The worst people made it; it was produced, as the story went, like the seed inside them. From bad milk comes bad fat. The girl ended up there from good seed, but inside she was a deceiver. Picked up as a runaway she was sent to work in the dairy plant. One morning, after the horrors I have partially relayed here, she ducked out before her roll call. Lived in the cracks, in the rows of tall blocks near the sewers, where the drug dealers and the addicts, the pimps and the whores worked. Her family had lost touch with her, and she felt hopeless.

These women were my stock-in-trade. I shan't titillate you with the details she recounted to me in some confidence. What I recount to you is to illustrate the change in me that found in her, in spite of all this, a worthy companion.

Among this destitution, she lived for men. For their crueller affections she satisfied their needs, and for her basest needs she fucked whoever could supply her. That's all. I'll admit, I was quite disgusted to hear the specifics of these stories, and when she told me of how she spread her legs for them, how she arched her back like an animal as they took her, two at a time, I was angry, angry first at them, and then, yes, at her. Yet even when faced with my reaction, she showed no shame, only regret. There was nothing, I suppose, that she hadn't already worked through in her mind, no shame she hadn't yet felt, processed, and surpassed. I could hardly be angry at that.

One night, she said, she was taken by so many, many men she could no longer count, and lost herself to the sensations where they made contact with her orifices, her ears, her organs. After that night she felt pregnant: the child was not of a single father but of many, many fathers. And as she spoke into the flames of our fire, the flames spoke back. The Devil, I saw, had breathed his own life into that baby, and in the licks of flame there appeared the poisonous child within her womb, made of a myriad of men.

She lost the child to the city. She gave birth to him, and they took him – not the city authorities but other men – and she didn't have the strength to resist. The eyes within the flames spoke clear enough to me, for their sight is omniscient.

'The child,' I told her, 'still lives in the city. But do not go back for him. You are well rid of him . . .' She finished my sentence for me: 'For he is the Antichrist.'

What is this allegory that we told together? Of sin carnate, born in flesh, passed down as a curse in the seed of the father, or fathers? What purpose could it serve, but to fulfil some Old Testament prophecy?

The old worlds must make way for a new universe of meaning, born free of the fairy tales that kept women such as her chained to the crucible, drenched in mould. In my migration, I didn't discover a new world; it came to meet me as I moved through it, surrounding my soul.

'These old tales,' I whispered to her, as she lay down to sleep. 'These old tales aren't told in these hills. Here they talk of the trees. As young saplings they shoot up in growth. But it is only when they bud, with the wisdom of age, that they flower.' I traced my finger across her skin, where the tattoos were raised like scars. 'We are made in His image, and all our sins are His. What is of significance lies behind the phenomena we can see – the eyes in the flame, the men in the caves, the wind upon the plain. The phenomena are manifestations of that deeper, common law. Who is your child? He is of God.'

> *O noblest green viridity,*
> *You're rooted in the sun*
> *and in the clear*
> *bright calm*
> *you shine within a wheel*
> *no earthly excellence*
> *can comprehend:*

You are surrounded by
the embraces of the service,
the ministries divine.

As morning's dawn you blush,
as sunny flame you burn.

XI

OUR BOND WAS transforming. I still fed her first, and she watched me while she ate, greedily. At night she no longer slept facing me. Indeed, she turned further away, and sometimes we shared no heat at all. Perhaps I was imagining it, but I felt her resent my resistance to the temptations she knew too well, as if she were a little bitter, or as if I had made her senseless through rejection. We didn't – couldn't – talk to each other about what had passed between us in the farmhouse that night. These unspoken tensions brewed into a kind of poison, to the point that I considered offering back something of what she offered me. But my temptations . . . they were not so much of the flesh, more of other intimacies. At times, I felt like reaching over to touch her hand in the night would be a comfort that might be appreciated. Yet it was she who moved away from me, and that distance between our breathing bodies was enough to hold me back.

It is possible, of course, that I was reading too much into this. In these matters, I was the novice and she the superior, with her understanding of the subtle movements of power and desire. As we moved across the countryside, the weather also changed: heat was stored in the soil, and without a breeze we sweated through the night almost as much as during the day. Perhaps that's why she didn't want to be too close to me.

This new landscape was alien to me. The fields of wheat were replaced by red, dusty hills and scrubland, which we paced for days, with no elevation to see out further than the next hill, or the next. Deep rivulets were scored in the earth by streams and the odd irrigation canal, where we would stop to refill our water flasks. Our hair, our eyelashes, our skin and our clothes became caked in a fine layer of arid soil. We shifted our routine, waking earlier, before the first shards of dawn, and walking until midday. Then we would try to find some shade and sleep for three or four hours when the sun was at its peak.

Such heat sharpens the senses. Some nights the clicking of cicadas was ear-splitting, while during the day, driven into a trance by the walking, the sound of an animal in the undergrowth or a hawk calling overhead could startle you. The smells were intoxicating. I tried to ensure that she, we, ate enough – something of what we had managed to forage before entering this tract of ruddy summer land, and what we could pull from the trees – bitter, unripe olives, and succulent oranges, so tart you could only eat a couple a day, lest they upset the humours and bring up acidic yellow bile.

On one of our rest stops, I ripped the blanket I had stolen from the farmhouse in two to make a scarf for each of us, a loose veil to keep the inexorable sun, dust and flies from our faces.

The scarf was bundled up beneath my head as a cushion that afternoon, as I lay against the roots of a gnarled olive tree, recharging before our evening trek. My over-tuned senses began to tremble. I could hear the dry leaves shaking, as if in the wind, but the air was still. She was asleep, curled up like a cat beneath another tree, so I stood up to see what was afoot. Two groves away a cloud of dust was accumulating, leaving a long tail in its swirling path. The cause of the dust, I couldn't see, but I could feel it beneath me. The earth, as well as the trees, was shuddering. I lifted myself up onto the olive's knotted trunk, then grabbed hold of a branch and climbed high up into it. I was above the height of the trees, and from here I could make out that around the cloud there was more movement, and within the cloud too, and I could hear noises. Human noises, impenetrable but intentional, calling to each other in full voices.

I can't tell you how moving that moment was: it wasn't just the cacophony but the whole scene, bathed in a rich goldenness. This clarity of light and energy gave me a hope that had felt impossible – from the burning morning of the first last day, through the forests and the broken nights and the storms and panic and baseness. I was aflame with the idea of what this cloud might present. I thought it was different and therefore *good*, yet the notion that novelty would bring promise was quite ridiculous, given what had come before. Nevertheless, seeing this leviathan progress across the earth, I felt a glow spread through me, from my blistered feet, tensed on the olive branch, into my cheeks, which were smeared with red-grey soil.

I stumbled and hopped down the branches, shouting at the girl: 'Hey, hey – go, come!' She woke dozily, unused to any haste in my voice, a change from the plodding routine of our lives.

'Wha?'

'Come! Here, a leviathan, far off!'

I gestured at the rolling dust cloud, bundled together my clothes, and pushed my feet back into my brittle leather boots. She rose to her feet to get a glimpse. From the ground all we could see were the first wisps of the cloud, but she was just as excited as I was for what it might hold, and collected up her things swiftly so we could go. Slipping down the bank and running up the other side, back into the olive grove, I went one way, she the other. As we neared we could pick out from within the rumbling specific sounds: a high pipe riding a familiar melody, some peasant song, and beneath it, the slow thud of hand drums. I paused, and unsheathed my knife, and hissed at the girl, who did not hear me and kept up her cheerful pace.

'Stop,' I hissed again, and she turned around. I pulled her into a crouch behind the stone wall of the olive grove. We were at the boundary; beyond was a few hundred metres of clear, open country, cut through by a wide track leading over a bridge made from rocks. The cloud was coming straight towards us.

'It comes,' I said to her. 'We see.'

As the cloud drew closer, we saw a host of people crowding inside. The first to emerge were two ranks of men, twenty or thirty of them wearing leather boots bound with rope up their sturdy calves and leather tabards punctured with metal bolts. Huge leather straps were wrapped around their waist and shoulders, connecting each man to the next man, and each man to an immense tree trunk that lay between their two rows. They heaved the central beam with all their might, while others carried staves, billhooks and pitchforks. Some had dogs on leashes, others were dressed in the habits of religious orders, grey, brown and black. All the men were locked in this labour, devoted to the great stake, oblivious of the world surrounding them.

The girl poked her head above our stone parapet. 'See,' she said, pointing towards the top of the brownish cloud. I looked where she indicated. I could make out the tips of two flags, one pink and one crimson, faded from the sun. Over the sound of the music and the commotion, you could hear the creaking of wood. All of a sudden, all pandemonium broke loose. The men knelt to rid themselves of the leather straps, and then from within the cloud more men, and now women, carrying wooden ladders, which they lifted up and then dropped back into the cloud, before falling to the ground with exhaustion. A large barrel was rolled out, and the men were given bowls of water to pour over their heads and wash off the sweat and grime.

The dust that had been churned began to settle, or else blow off above the olive groves in curls. A gargantuan cart became visible, a haywain towering up above its workers. The girl turned to me, stunned by this caravan of human endeavour. It must have been forty metres in length with eight cartwheels on each side, twice as high as the tallest man. The base of the wagon was level with the heads of those dragging it by a shaft that jutted out from the front. It was an open warehouse for an entire colony: a mountain of goods and bushels were piled on top; stacks of tightly packed hay bales with hemp ropes to hold them teetering in place. Among the bales were over-sized crates of squawking chickens and peacocks, geese and goats, and sheaves of found metals (railway tracks, ironing boards, car doors). There were reels of copper wire and rolls of tarpaulin, and tools and knives hanging from the sides. The thin ladders ran up to the wide platform, and up and down scooted the hay men, throwing ropes or pulling goods out for their brief stop. Atop the juggernaut were planks and slats on which passengers were seated, garbed in clothing I'd never seen in the city: oddly hooded capes, cigarette pants with clunky boots; monks' or nuns' robes, turbans and tunics.

I guessed that these people must have been a self-sufficient community prior to the Judgement, and made their decision to depart in good time, fabricating the wieldy engine as the vehicle of their solidarity. We looked on for a while as they fed their few cattle, lashed to the haywain at the rear, and watered them from the stream. Perhaps, I began to think, the leviathan could offer some material salvation for the two of us. I looked in my bag: not much left – a couple of bags of dried beans, a tin of preserved fish. I watched the haymaker's band break apart their bread, just steps from our foxhole. I worried I couldn't care for the girl much longer. What options did we have? We were nearing starvation, walking further into the wilderness.

The sun was starting its gradual descent in the sky when the commotion picked up again. The girl was snoozing beside me under its afternoon heat. I shook her awake and her eyes flashed open.

'Ready yourself,' I warned her.

It was a lurching start. As well as the ranks of men bound to its forward staff, all spare hands were assigned to four ropes, attached just afore the four axles. When the horn sounded, they heaved on the ropes, attempting to pull the wheels out of a rut. The cart would shift, seeming to move forward, before falling back in, and the motion would begin again, until the whole vessel rocked like a baby's crib. Eventually some momentum was achieved and the charabanc began its journey, with its many feet and its fluttering flags stirring the almighty cloud. As the giant began to disappear into the dust, I grabbed the girl by the shoulder and we stumbled out of our hiding place towards it. It was now picking up speed, and those not already aboard were the fittest and strongest, assigned to gathering the last of the ropes. I held her hand tightly as we slipped as fast as we could over the loose, dry earth. The noise of the creaking wheels, crunching on the rocks, was deafening. We ran between a group of men, and they shouted at us to get up, get up. I reached for the ladder through the choking grit, at first struggling to grip it, but then managed to pull my foot up, finding my balance. The girl reached for another ladder, a few paces behind. I thought for a second that she was going to miss; the colossal wheel was rolling faster as the cart began to descend towards the bridge. She was in danger of being dragged beneath, but just as I feared it, she reached out boldly and clung to the rung. I leaned back and grabbed her other arm, hauling her aboard, when she let out a howl and a shot of bright red blood spurted to the floor moving beneath us. The vehicle was shaking, and we still had another ladder to climb up the side of the hay bales. I looked to where she had leapt up on the cart: an iron spike poked out of the wood, red with her blood, and seeping into the rope that had been looped around it.

'Hold me!' I shouted, over the snapping of the wheels. I began to launch myself and the girl up the next ladder, until she could get her good leg firmly onto a rung. One of the rope men had climbed up the ladder beside us and relieved me of our bundled bags. We were halfway up the side, but I now had to lift her body the remainder of the way as the cart began to cross the bridge. I couldn't avoid looking down, to ensure her feet were secure, which filled me with a violent swaying sensation – to sense the fall to the bridge, and then the fall to the dry ravine down below. I might at any moment drop her to her death, I thought, after all this time. Somehow, we reached the top of the stack, whereupon people took her by the arms and wrenched her up onto the planks. I followed.

I unholstered my knife and sliced straight up her trouser leg, knotted a makeshift tourniquet, and tied it just above her knee. The men stood around us in disgusted shock – at the blood, at the sight of us women, who knows. The women knelt next to me in an instant. One handed me a terracotta jug of cool water so I could clean up the leg. One wiped the dripping sweat from the girl's pallid forehead. She did not look good.

So much for becoming secret stowaways. Yet no one accosted us; the girl's health was in danger, and so they let me tend to her, aiding me where they could.

I washed my hands in the jug of water and began to inspect her wound. I felt woozy – the rush of adrenaline from the climb and the vertigo of the drop, the rocking motion of the cart in the heat . . . The gash was just above her right knee and as long as my hand span. As I turned her onto her side she wailed and the twisted flesh exposed raw bone beneath. I used two fingers on each hand to tease the slit apart and see if any dirt had got in. I looked deep into the wound, which appeared to blur, then glow, through the stifling air, which stung my eyes. I touched the torn edge of her flesh in order to clean it, and she winced, cried out, and buckled against me.

'Hold!' I yelled at the women, not knowing what language they spoke. The girl swung the flat back of her hand at me with all her might, and I parried the blow with my arm. Two women held the girl down to the boards by her shoulders, pinning her arms. A man put his knees either side of her ears, and used a leather band as a bit, which he forced between her unwilling teeth. My head, by now parched and starved of sugars, salts and air, pounded painfully. The front felt like it was swelling. Through the dust cloud the towering silhouettes of the peasants seemed backlit by a mysterious glow. I supped at length from the water jug.

Inside the wound, I could see tiny pieces of glass and stone, and the very tip of the rusted iron prong. If I didn't remove it, it would poison her blood and kill her by sunrise. The bleeding was abating, but infection posed a great risk.

Inside, I could see everything – all the workings of life revealed. A shard of light split my sight in two, tearing vision from vision, knowledge from knowledge. In the simplest of ways, I tried to read what the wound was saying, and let its teachings flow into me through the blinding splinter of light.

The wound bulged at the bottom then widened like an egg, before tapering at the top. The lip, where the skin had ripped, was a flaming ring. White hot fire licked up the split epidermis over a darkened rim of scarlet flame. This fire burned with such intensity that even within the thickening dust cloud the whole wound was illuminated. The outer flames would blow and spark, one way and then the other, as though the wind was rapidly changing, and beneath the two layers, the light dimmed to yet another layer of fire, this gloomier than the others. In the centre of the voluminous void, a perfectly spherical globe of auburn fire was revealed. Above the globe, which vibrated with life, were three torches, aglow with flame.

In this occult haze I found myself drawn into the layers of fire. I moved my head closer to the wound, which pulsated, and emitted an icy crash, as if an avalanche was falling through her bloody flesh. Set against this sound, the clattering of the wagon and the industry of its villagers fell to silence. All else dissipated.

The limit of my vision was the wound. It seemed blessed, as Christ's wound was blessed: a slit, not cut through the girl's leg but through the veil that separates this world from the next. It was imminent death made manifest into an eternal future; she would have disappeared through that wound if I had let her. It was just me and the wound, and behind the wound, the girl, and inside the wound, the world. In the wound was the universe, as it existed in real and material things, and in the wound was the universal truth, essential meaning. Here, now, things simply *were*, in and of themselves, and this was enough and this was everything. From these fiery lips, life in its purest form spoke to me.

I plunged the index finger of my right hand into the weeping hole. A hurricane of energy whirled around the globe, bringing with it a torrent of water, which evaporated in an instant and infiltrated the

atmosphere as a vapour. I pressed harder, channel-
ling all of my self into this divine mystery. Within the
lips, I was purified in my true faith. While the devilish
darkness of the lowest levels of wavering fire brought
confusion, the torches communicated with me directly
– uncommunicable thoughts, not words nor ideas but
ways of seeing and being.

All moments were within this one. Everything is
of itself, in itself, its own self, its itsness: the holiest
mystery of all. The words of my grandfather's Old
Testament came tumbling back. Where they spoke
of *the generations of the heavens and of the earth when
they were created*, I saw the girl's body, laid out before
me, covered in her blood, and I saw it too, in the
cool waters of the stream where she had first cleaned
herself of the forest's filth. *But there went up a mist from
the earth, and watered the whole face of the ground. And the
Lord God formed man of the slime of the earth, and breathed
into his face the breath of life; and man became a living soul.*

Around my finger the fire of life throbbed. I felt
its voice and lowered my head further towards the
wound, which began again to bleed, a trickle of the
thickest blood. The single stream ran down my finger
to escape the sliced flesh. I pushed my tongue against
the ball of my palm and began to lick, drinking her
blood as it gushed forth, until my mouth tasted of

the iron spike that had made this opening. My teeth stained pink, I did not care about the women gathered around me. I was absorbed in the communion of her flesh as the poisons drained from her body and I took them into mine. The moment was holy and profane; it gave expression to the terrible suffering of man; for we are made in His image and my violence is but a feeble aspect of His Judgement.

She screamed, and I knew from this piercing tone that her body was finally clean. I bound her wound tightly in white linen, handed to me from a nursemaid among the crowd, and, exhausted by this exorcism, wiped my mouth clean of her blood. Between the city walls and this place, I had been reduced.

PART III

XII

MY WORK OF HEALING that they now regarded as holy had, at the time, seemed utterly ungodly. An act of witchcraft, my drinking from the wound, from the Devil's cup. When my doubled fingers penetrated the hood of her skin and touched the globe, it was, in truth, a vision of the earth in the moment of creation. I had become connected to the power of our creator.

I have no doubt that their slovenly priest, who looked on from his seat in front of the haywain guzzling wine, would have sucked us dry given half a chance. The day of the girl's accident, I was wary that the rough villagers riding the cart would do the same, or worse, feasting on us. Who could blame the peasants who observed the scene? Two strange women arriving without welcome with a scene of bloody carnage and a ritual that was far from the rote Eucharists of their own greedy holy man. Had she died, I would have been thrown under the wain to be crushed on the track under its awesome wheels, my body turned to carrion for vultures. Thank God, then, that sheer shock disabled them from knowing what to do with me. I lay exhausted and wrapped in my blanket, sound asleep in the soft straw, as the cart continued to trundle through the night. By the time I awoke, the girl was already up; her fever had gone down thanks to my action, and she smiled sweetly at the nursemaids who had adopted her. As such, I was taken not as a witch but as a miracle worker. For my labours I became their mascot.

The next day the priest demanded I appear before him for a drumhead court-martial. But the haywainers rallied round me, speaking in my defence in rowdy voices. I could see, perhaps for the first time, a quiver of fear passing over his eyes. He, the one who was delivering them, preferred his flock subdued, patiently awaiting his command. He demanded their subservience, yet here they were, making demands of his authority by asking for mercy to be given to me.

A weak man, he buckled with an angry dismissal; I was to be allowed to continue with the group, but as a milkmaid, no more. Any nursing role was prohibited, much less any healing. As for the girl, she was to be brought before him when she was better. I worried for her fate, but there was little I could do in the meantime. As I had thought, the people were from a farming village in the hinterlands. They had operated in the antiquated way, paying their tithe to the Church and their wealth to the Duke. These fiefdoms still existed then, but only on the outer edge of the city's influence where it held little authority. In the immediate aftermath of Judgement Day, that way of life began to come under threat, and this tyrannical pot-boiler of a priest knew it. The agricultural provinces were burning under thundering clouds, and with that future emerging, he planned to keep his authority by moving the people themselves. Moses, Exodus, it was all there on paper, the better for him to utilise. His lieutenants, seconded from the Duke, exercised their rights, and the company of refugees began their march.

Between themselves, the villagers talked about their fate. There was no love for the pastor, only fear, but there was hope for what he preached. A journey towards another place, where the land was more fertile than the rocky soil of their village. There, like the city of the Tafurs I had hoped to find, poverty was rewarded by God. Their stories soon began to win me over. I believed their tales of the new city, and even began to embellish them, as if I had already seen the utopian metropolis with my own eyes. And what a city it was, with public baths and theatres, and joyous festivals, and stadia, and endless markets that would be hungry for the villagers' goods. Each night we built the city out of our hopes. It became real: we would be thrilled with each discovery, each previously unknown place where life could flourish in urbane comfort. I started to imagine what life I would make when I got there. A simple life, I decided. I might one day forget the horrors I had fled, forget the before as well as the after, which still shook me awake at night. Maybe the girl could live nearby, and find herself free too. The day in which we met the Tafurs could not come quick enough; I prayed for their fair hand in the promised land.

Now we weren't the only refugees. Sometimes, over the evening's fire, we would talk in hushed tones about what had happened, and the villagers would listen aghast – not just at what we had lost, but at what we had in the first place. We had something that they couldn't share: the trauma of destruction and loss. The girl and I, and others like us, could never truly belong to the wagons. Our lives had begun too differently, so we formed a discrete band within them.

The late summer gave way to the rainy season. It made the going tough; the cartwheels regularly got stuck in the mud, and we could spend whole afternoons trying to lever ourselves out of the ruts with ropes and duckboards. In the evenings we struggled to cook, as our fires spewed plumes of dense white smoke from the wet wood. Left untended, by the morning they would be drenched to the cinders. The earth was dampened – with the blanket of olive leaves, fallen branches and dead twigs soaked through, the sounds of the forest were muffled and muted. The long nights of cricket serenades, a rare moment of pleasure, died with our sick.

And that's how they got me. Coming into a sheltered wood, a handful of us leapt off the wagon to find dry kindling for the fires, which had been starved of fuel for so long that we too had made do with poor sustenance. I had no sense of any others around besides our party, as I crouched down, intent on my task of gathering twigs. A broad and leathery hand clasped my mouth, another choked my throat and dragged me backwards into the unseen territory. My mind entered a delirium, and I passed into the night.

I awoke in a darkness so black I wasn't sure I was truly conscious. The lingering effects of their poison – the bitterest herbs sweetened with honey, I am sure – heightened the sensation of being a stranger to myself. Captivity transforms you. The limits of what you can know shrink to the four walls in which you are kept, and with nothing but darkness to give definition to what exists in actuality, you find other passageways of experience. Lines of flight.

It was here, in the dark prison of a tent where one foot could touch each wall, that I began journeying further. I shall share with you the travels of my mind as my flesh was held captive. Light reflects off the worldly things, and gives them shape and form to our eyes. Those shapes and forms occupy our mind, in the attempt to spot the movement of a predator or the silhouette of the prey. In the city, I had spent my life busied with the natural tendency to look for patterns in phenomena, obsessed with the administration of order. Without light, touch or taste – without a world – there is only inner life to encounter. This brings sweetness and madness in equal measure. Imprisoned, I travelled across distance and through time. I found myself in the landscapes of my childhood, and there I found solace in the times it would have been easier to die. What follows is my childhood story, which has so far gone untold, for it was buried; it is only human to turn away from pain and lock away the primal losses of our tenderest years.

I grew up not far from the city walls, but legally speaking, outside them. The culture was markedly different there. We lived in a collection of houses spread across the bottom of a valley, along an ancient road that had run deep into the soil over its centuries of existence. From the road, tracks led up onto the mountainside to small enclaves of farms. We would walk up to visit my mother's friends and their families in these high farmhouses of a few buildings set around a yard. When the light failed me, these forms I saw and these impressions I felt: The late summer's final fruits in a mess of thorny bushes. Her hands stained pink and purple from their juices, holding mine as we walked the last few kilometres up the stony tracks. The smell of the pines we stopped under, while she dropped to her knees to pull a splinter from my thumb. And the heat, the heat. I was in the valley with my mother; the sun and sweat of my memories were just as real as the damp and mildew of the tent.

My mother made cheese. That is important, you will remember. She wasn't just a cheesemaker. She was someone who could transform all the harvests of our dry valley into richness, like most of the men and women who scratched a living from that silty soil. Magicians of everyday life. I didn't only meet my mother, and taste her fresh cheese again in my prison. I was also taken back to the morning I first saw the Devil.

The Devil finds you alone. I could sense his presence as I walked through the hollow in the shade of the stone bridge. He thrives where there is no light, this wild adversary, who is not sulphurous as much as a rising damp, a black mould that grows within. I felt disturbed, seized by an almost violent urge, which froze me in place. The water beside me slowed, until it too stood still. First clockwise and then anti-clockwise, the water twisted and stirred up the muddy riverbed until it became a stew of molasses, growing blacker and blacker until it was void of all light. The branches of the trees contorted in the wind, old boughs releasing great groans. A painful sensation ascended from my gut, making me feel like I would vomit from my depths. I was stirred into a wildness. If I had had an iron bar I would have smashed everything in my reach. I was panicked, but at the same time, a physical joy buoyed me. From the spitting water he rose, the White Terror, splashing the bridge's side, evil on high. I saw his face and I was made in his image, and the power and fury that had drawn him from the darkness smelled good to me. I broke free of my torpor, and began to run from the dark knowing it would be useless. He had caught my scent and was on my heels, and from that young morn I would spend my life trying to evade him.

It was months before I told my mother. When she asked why I didn't tell her before, I replied, 'I thought you'd think I was lying.' She kissed me on the forehead. 'Of course not. I knew he would find you soon enough. I just hoped we'd have a few more years.' Her eyes were damp, but she didn't seem sad. 'Don't worry,' she said, holding me tight. 'Keep faith in light and he won't catch up with you.'

Many years later, even after she sent me away, creating a wound, a distance, between us, I still returned to those words. 'Keep faith in light,' I would tell myself each morning when I woke from another night troubled by my lungs and my worries. Some days the Devil crept into the dark corners of my apartment. Some days I could feel him, shadowing me, and his presence was comforting in its familiarity.

In my cold days of imprisonment, as the dampness turned to an ever-icier chill, he appeared more often, and at times I would have let him in. I was certainly tempted: by the promise of restoration to my life in the city, in my office; to my authority and the sense of order and satisfaction I got from my work. I was tempted to abandon my reason, which had guided me thus far. When I held back, I felt the deceiver shooting sharp pains at my liver.

The Devil had in his service my captors. The Tafurs. I heard them talking outside the tent, and recognised them before seeing them, by their words and deeds. They came to me to hang me from iron bars, shouting: 'Where is your kingdom now?' They tried to break my will with deprivation and torture – to smash my sanity so I would become one of those possessed by him. But I would not succumb and they punished me for it with countless more days of abyssal solitude, until the next time. Alone again, I would focus on my finger-tips, running them across the damp canvas walls and my open scars. My fingers were my connection to the senses and so to my life, destitute as it was. I knew where I was and who I was. There was no one these Tafurs hated more, rude cannibals, than symbols of the old order like me. But what was there left to extract from me?

The state of abjection contains within it the seed of transformation. My new soul would emerge and the Devil hated me for the brilliance of my rebirth. In the darkness, I had my vision.

I woke from fitful sleep, and went to touch my face, to trace its contours. At the front of my head was a throbbing pain, and I pushed the balls of my thumbs into my eyes, pulling down to stretch my lower eyelids and hold them open to the night. A small dot appeared before me: like a firecracker, it spat and sizzled insistently, and exploded into a larger ball of white hot magnesium, a nebula in microcosm, which consumed the darkness and cast my likeness in black on the wall of the tent. From this round galaxy burst forth another flame, which filled the room with a warmth like that of a set of candles offered in tribute at a church. Within this second flame was a third, ever-brighter light. It was the light of dawn, a lost and perfect dawn I remembered from my family's farmstead, breaking over the far hill one spring morning when I had risen early as a young girl, sleepily drawing back the barn doors to feed our hens. Inside the cell, a burning flame; inside that flame, a brighter flame; and inside that, a veritable dawn, which reflected off the tent floor, which was now bejewelled with topaz.

I pinned my back to the wall, raising my right arm to shield my face from the radiance. I could see my skeleton through my skin, but as I put my arm down I found I could look directly at the centre of the light without burning my eyes. Inside the dawn was a womb, and inside the womb was a person. The person was me: fully formed yet miniature, turning as the sphere contracted and dilated. Vibrations filled the tent, warming me as they travelled along my spine. Finally, the edges of the burning ball touched the sides of the womb and the whole of the fiery light poured itself into the tiny me, through the little skeleton, along the millions of nerves, illuminating the lymphatic system. The flesh appeared tender and supple, fat like the underarms. As it was animated by the energy that filled it, I knew that I would be made strong in its goodness. My nervous system filled with a sensation novel to me; I felt outside of my self – a feeling not unlike how I had felt as a child beneath the bridge as the Devil revealed himself to me. The roaring wind that accompanied his presence whipped around the space, but I did not waver; I stood on the spot in silence, watching myself in the womb. I knew that this time he could haunt me no longer.

But what did it benefit the Devil to be opposed to me? The Devil wished to be very bright and to be elevated above all things. The other proud spirits agreed with the Devil. My divine power with the strength of righteousness cast them out all together.

To know that I was loved and was worthy of love. This did not make the pain much easier to bear, in fact, it made it harder, this final absence, when the only person I had to face in my cell was myself. But the light had provided enough strength to rebuild my soul. For years I carried the regret of the sorrow I must have caused for my mother. Her organ's appearance revived me like a hot brandy poured into the mouth of a dying soul. It was a strong and honeyed reminder of life, which I had almost lost touch with. My mother's words, to keep faith in light, tasted as sweet to me as that burnished gold on my lips. With this, I was released from the prison of my own making, which had kept so much pain, so much grief, in my knotted stomach. It was not the cuts and burns to my flesh that dressed my body, but the words of my mother that released from me enough tears to wash my wounds. Then, the light sucked itself back, exiting the tiny body, the sphere, the room, the wind receding with it.

In the remaining time in that cell I realised that my identity was only as strong as those who understood it. Without identity, I had only the light, which sometimes receded to the faintest glimmer. I relearned my relationship to the world through the touch of my fingertips on the damp cage and through the bursts of brightness between the synapses of my brain, and there I found truth. To live is to see afresh, to die is to be held down at the stake of the past.

They would then put down the oldness of ignorance and take up the newness of life.

They abandoned the camp overnight. One morning I was dragged from my canvas cell into the open air, to find the remains of a camp turned upside down on the barren land. I was sure that I and the other prisoners would be executed. Somehow we were spared. Most of the partisans had left, and were already trekking up into the hills. Sitting around huddled in the boiler suits they had made us wear, I could see the evidence of their bestial treatment in their bestial behaviour. One woman dug into the earth with intent, as if she had buried something there, but she uncovered nothing but soil, which clung to her fingers and got stuck beneath her nails. The more she dug, the more infuriated she grew. Her frustrated grunts disturbed me, as did her erratic fury. I ran over to her and struggled to top her, to pull her back from her hole. For a moment she resisted. I feared she would bite me, but then she relented and collapsed back into my arms and I held her. I tried to speak to her but she didn't understand my language. My words were sticking inside my mouth as if it were coated in treacle. I realised I wasn't speaking, not really; my tongue was twisted. When she spoke, I couldn't understand her either. We shared nothing more than the violence we had suffered. I left her, and rummaged through the upturned camp, salvaging a torn overcoat, then set off into the woods. Following the tracks left by the departing Tafurs' sleds, I walked for hours until I was high above the smouldering ruins of the camp, visible only from the trails of smoke that rose from it. How many months had I spent there? What pains had been inflicted? I paused and made a promise: I would not dwell on the violence, only on what I had restored.

XIII

THE LAND CRADLED my onward journey, as I walked away from that dark detention. I came to believe, indeed, that I had been kidnapped by the very people I had hoped would save me. The cruelty of this band and the poverty of their encampment made me wonder if this was the origin of the rumours of the Tafur Kings, masters of the dispossessed. What foolishness to assume in their poor desperation there would be a place for a refugee like me. It seemed to have been sheer luck that something had moved them on before I could become another victim of their hunger, a hunger that drove them in pillage and rapine. They knew no restraint, I later heard, and would even pull the dead from their graves to eat them.

I could no longer sleep in the dark, so I reversed my routine, progressing onward at night, recalling as I walked the city's brilliant nightlife. The legion dangers of the night were guarded against with vigilance, while during the day I slept like a child in the afternoon, with the greenness as my nursemaid. I passed for perhaps ten nights through the primordial woods, the undergrowth kept low only by nature's maintenance, never having seen an arboriculturist. Some days I had to beat through the dense foliage for hours; other days I made pleasant progress through open vales and clearings, free from thorns and bandits, populated with fawns and a gentle breeze. After the forest came a scrubland of tight gorse bushes bloomed with a coconut scent, and thickets of rosemary and thyme over rocky ground. This landscape spread for miles, drifting down to an unknown shore. It never rained during this period of walking, so I drank from thin streams deep in the rock, and scavenged what meagre provisions I could. As the land descended, I cut down into a narrow canyon to stay nearer to the fresh water. At its bottom there was more shade for me to sleep in during the day, a little more moisture to collect at night, and ripe fruit trees. Gazing up into the cloudless sky I could see every star, my passage drawn beneath their firmament. I was new to this city of lights, a young woman, recently arrived, captivated by the illuminated boulevard that hung in a line above my head.

Those pure spring days, where a hint of warmth begins to penetrate the soil at last, activating the spores and moulds and mosses that will soon fill the forest air with a proliferation of life; those spring days, the mild breeze and the earth's scents blow through your memories, stirring a resurrection within you.

There was something renewed in me: the nagging pains had subsided, and I was not plagued by remorse. With no right of return and no future ahead, I was nearing the climax of the pass, with only snow-covered tops above me. This was the true threshold, for which I had broken through the city walls, healed the sick, climbed and scaled and thought and felt and reimagined, in order to reach. This was the undrawn border on the map. The solitary journey through landscape is one of personal discovery, and as I gained altitude each day, my relationship with the self rose too.

This transliteration between word and thing underpins every vision I have, whether real or fantastical. This transmutation is the very path we walk when we move out of one relationship, with ourselves, or with the world, and into another. Perhaps to others, this slow unfolding seems quite dull, and after the fact, like an obvious destiny. The absence of innovation is a vital element for telling our stories to ourselves. The urge to innovate – to make things up, anew – is within us all, as doctors, writers or travellers. But this urge is far from pure, and a million pilgrims can walk the same tracks through the countryside and all arrive in different places. In fact it is through the pilgrim's path, the pedestrian ways, that we must discover our relationships to things in themselves, within the mundanity of our daily life, as it is everyday life that must be transformed. It was only in the violence of my separation from my past life, in the trauma of loss, and with this time for reflection, that I came to this realisation. I know not why; I still do not know what is wrong with me. But what is wrong with me is *me*, that much is true. My temptation to sin was based on this self, and cannot be erased, only known as it is. The forest taught me this too – to feel with my fingers, and to recognise what I felt.

Each step across the quilt of the forest floor felt like I was eight years old again, back in the city-centre church dedicated to the Holy Mother. There was so much about that church, its rituals, and the monsters who crept along the cloisters, that filled me with fear. They were such tedious terrors for a child to endure – not so much the fear of God, but of halitosis and fingers that pinched all parts of the body. This was a place of holy blood, but the holy blood had been painted over with one hundred generations of sticky brown varnish that must, I thought, have choked the Holy Mother and her Child. It was as if the heavy wood from which the figures of the Holy Mother and her newborn infant were carved were still squeezing a viscous sap from between each ring. I wondered how long ago they broke her image free of the forest. What happened in the decade between breast and brow? Within the darkened cathedral walls her flesh could never grow warm beneath sunlight.

'Watch,' my grandfather whispered in my ear. 'They will hoist the censer.' The priest would open a casket and pick up a silver hand shovel, like that of a confectioner. He would plunge it into the box and pull out a shovelful of incense, which he would drop into the censer's silver bowl of hot coals. The priest fastened it shut and the man on the rope hoisted it into its swinging arc above our heads, where it would glow in the cathedral's gloom. The smell was a musky miasma, like lifting a horse's saddle after a day in the hills. The sweetness of myrrh and the dank odour of the arriving pilgrims, with their pustulating blisters and acrid sweat, mingled to lift up the rest of the congregation. The spiritual labours of the pilgrims were of life, unlike the creosoted statues. Between the growth of the pilgrim's soul and the slow decay of the flesh, there was holy worship.

With each pace through the forest, the abundance of the worm-ridden earth and the dry incense of fallen pine needles fused to take me back to the church, and this combination of decomposition and transcendence. Hundreds of metres ahead, I could see movement: the shivering silver of a modest lake. The water was sparkling and fresh and I buckled to it without volition, leaning face first until my nose touched the surface, then lifting it to my lips with both hands. It tasted so clear I felt I could drink for forever, and I nearly did, lying there on the bank until my arms began to ring with pins and needles.

I went to the water, and I was quenched. We scale our desires to our circumstances: Who would have thought that simply washing my hands in the purest water, and drinking deeply from it, would create in me a feeling of absolute contentment? That this would allow, for just an hour, the sensations that had come to constitute my bodily life – the raw flesh of my palms, cracking knees, and swollen cuts – to dissipate. The merest of clouds collected on the edge of the horizon; above was an azure that, along with the thin air, was a symptom of high altitude. Soon the trees would fall away, soon the delicate flowers would spring up on the grassy slopes, the lilacs, yellows and pinks of primula and chamois ragwort, rock jasmine, bachelor's button and, of course, my favourite and most blessed, the darling edelweiss, 'Star of the Alps', the lion's paw.

The sun began to have a soporific effect as its rays played against my body. Before I knew it, like a napping child, I crossed out of this reality and into slumber. What trust we place in the world when we sleep. Lapsed from consciousness, we leave our bodies open and vulnerable to the world. Meanwhile we reawaken unprotected in a dim half-world, our souls susceptible only to our selves. Here I was unarmed, as around my corpse birds flew and sang.

The ground was covered in a generous layer of moss, which made for a comfortable bed. As I drifted off, it was as though the roots of the trees in which I nestled were growing around my body, not binding but rather cocooning me in their ark of wood. Here I was protected, not from the animals of the forest, for I too was an animal of the forest, but from the animals of the city, the republic and the regime. For them, for my life, I had been prey, and yet now the greenness in which I resided sustained me, in all ways, for my pilgrimage from city to shining city, until the end, as it was upon me.

I had reached a point of death, my young body broken. The roots of the tree crept around me, welcoming me home to the earth. My breathing became shallow. Each joint and each tendon ached, each twitch sent razors through my blood vessels. Crystals bloomed on the bone. The humours within me seemed to thicken and clot. I felt the light seep from my eyes and grew colder around the chest. I was aware of the texture of time shifting, as the light turns to dusk. I had turned to this wilderness in delinquency, expecting my journey to be an arduous crossing. Yet at every turn it was the forest and the water, the fields and the mountains, which supported me. Nature offered succour through viciousness and blood; the wind and storm carved the path across the land for me. I was pushed on by the forces of man and history, and found in the transgression of nature not a screaming void of the inhuman but a perpetual network of intelligence. The forest rots and grows, no different to me; it reaches out to touch me without guile. It is harsh and complex, mild and benevolent, all at once. The forest and the beings within and around it are fellow souls. Friends, made animate and equal by the greening power that is the spark and sustenance of creation in this vast web, this intergalactic ecosystem that connects all matter and the processes of life, death and rebirth. For to be born is to die and to die is to be reborn, and in my last moments in my waking state, I felt my pulse connect with the vibrations of all the life-forms around me to become unified waves, moving towards an ecstatic peace.

O noblest green viridity,
You're rooted in the sun
and in the clear
bright calm
you shine within a wheel
no earthly excellence
can comprehend:

You are surrounded by
the embraces of the service,
the ministries divine.

As morning's dawn you blush,
as sunny flame you burn.

XIV

I EXPECTED TO DIE, and death came, and yet passed over me. I slept through the evening and into the darkness. That night I dreamed only of the good and the dead, and in the night the sun appeared. *As the sun is the light of the day, so too the soul is the light of the waking body. And as the moon is the light of the night, so too the soul is the light of the sleeping body.* And so I slept with the sun and the soul as my sleeping lights.

The sun was of unimaginable brightness. It did not rise, but broke through the night direct from above. For a second, I could not place myself, and a dizziness came over me unlike any I had felt before, a flat plane of swirling static before my eyes. I felt terribly frightened but resisted the vertigo. Once I had broken through the frantic spinning, I could feel my self rising towards the burning sun, sitting among a field of luminous stars. I felt I was dying, but I had no fear of death; I must continue my pilgrimage through to the Republic of Souls.

Around me, the world turned white, absolutely white, as clear as the water that ran at my feet. All the world was like this – turned to water, but holding an immense, total white. From within the white, the girl emerged, as I had wished for her face from the moment my body was taken from me. She glowed – from her face to her breasts, a blushed gold, like early dawn, and from her breasts to her stomach, a noble purple, like a budding hyacinth. A heavy red tunic fell from her shoulders. I heard a heavenly voice say:

This flower on the heavenly Sion is the mother and flower of roses and the lily of the valleys.

Around the girl was a crowd of women. They were as radiant as the sun, bejewelled with gold and precious stones. Illuminated, I saw tattoos of a baby sheep, the Lamb of God, appear on their faces. The voice made the forest that surrounded me tremble and sway, as it pronounced:

These are the daughters of Sion, and with them are the ones who play their lyres with all the different musics, and who sing with total gladness and joy.

My heart was elated, but no sooner had they arrived, I saw, torn in the fabric of the girl's tunic, a window back to the worst of the city. Through the portal was a gloom so dark that my words cannot convey it – the falling towers, the dead, still hanging, the judged, still burning, the absolute destruction, the city taking joy in its own horror... My heart felt as though it were falling through my body with force, as if it, and I, might be sucked back through this window to the past. The voice now betrayed its deeper tones, a solemn horror of its own.

If the Word of God had not suffered on the cross, this darkness would not allow people to come to the heavenly light in any way.

I prepared to be tossed through the window, a treacherous return through time and space to my old sins. I tensed, but did not fear it. Here I have a warning for you.

All you who pass through this way, attend to and see if your sorrow is the same as my sorrow, because it vindicated me, as the Word spoke of the day of the Word's furious anger.

The air wrestled with my corpse and I was lifted to the window. As I made no attempt to resist, I was flung back to the ground before my girl, the furious light rendering me blind, and I took on all it offered me. The window closed; the girl's image faded.

I moved back across life's thinnest veil, back into my consciousness, where I inhabited my body again. I was exhausted, my head split in two from this light. The sun had dipped on its wheel in the sky, fingers of rays reaching across the heavens, to cast lengthy shadows from the forms of us on earth. From my troubled sleep I had emerged a little stronger. The air around me had a crystal clarity, the trees a sharp definition. How can I explain the difference? I felt, somehow, the history of this clearing as a place that had existed for eternity. Each wide tree had had a youth, each broken branch a tragedy, and I contemplated what that meant for me, a brief visitor to the ancient woodland, to carry away this moment I shared in its history.

Throughout my imprisonment, I had never known true silence. Even on the endless nights, cut off from the world, I had always been accompanied by a voice in my mind. I had considered that voice my own. I had heard it my whole life in the seminary and the city; I would guess that you know yours well too. It gripes and nags and soothes and cares, holding your hand, as it were, as you travel into unknown situations. The voice was not me. That voice is not you. The narrator is a fiction of the city. With the voice talking to me I could not hear nor speak His language. He may have tried to communicate with me via his visions, which I have interpreted for you in this text, but I had to leave to find His language. Now that the voice was gone, I listened to the silence of the pool's surrounds. In this silence, I found that for which I had left the city: He speaks to us silently in His unknown language of grace.

The sun sunk low enough that I could see no hard forms, just a silhouette of everything, all that light could not touch. Around the black outlines of life crept the golden light, and in my peace I thought of a proverb my grandfather had taught me when I was a slight and infirm child: 'From little acorns do mighty oaks grow.'

There was, indeed, a mighty oak. Yet set against the lustre of the sun, I sensed in my soul that my grandfather, in this rare instance, was wrong. The acorn, yes, gave its first seed to the forest. But too much emphasis is given to the moment of conception, of implantation into the earth. In the thousand years between that day and this, the oak did not simply grow, it was nurtured. Just like the edelweiss, legendary for its powers of healing. Just like the pine forest, the spelt and the cabbage; just like the bacteria that fed on them and on me; just as I was nourished. What gave the oak its strength? Not the acorn, blessed as the acorn is, but the energy of the sun. Nothing was missing from the nexus of the acorn's needs; God had provided everything. And what energy had gone into that mighty oak, had gone into the tiny edelweiss; what they had received from the sun's blessing was fungible. The oak could partake in the edelweiss' sun, and the edelweiss in the oak's, and both would thrive. What, then, was the difference between the might of the oak and the beauty of the edelweiss? None. They shared the same source of energy, and this same source revealed to me this divine truth of creation. I can think of no better word for that energy than grace.

He gave His energy to the oak, not for it to wither with limp leaves, and he gave the edelweiss its beauty, not for it to turn its face to the alpine stone. He gave to each, so that they may grow and blossom, and spread forth more evidence of His eternal and holy presence. That is, so that they could live. And be alive! *Ye are the light of the world. A city that is set on a hill cannot be hid.*

Are you looking for a critical eye in this vision? There is none – this is what separates my life outside the city from my life within the administration. I surrendered totally to the truth that was laid upon me. He tests His creation in every move, the better to glorify Him. The light that lives within you was not lit for you to dim it with your fears of a darkened world. *Take heed therefore that the light which is in thee be not darkness.*

And as the sun, the holiest energy, lay its fingers across my tanning brow, I accepted what it revealed to me, and lay down to live again in the light and greenness of God:

God is the foundation for everything
This God undertakes, God gives.
Such that nothing that is necessary for life is lacking.
Now humankind needs a body that at all times
honours and praises God.
This body is supported in every way through the earth.
Thus the earth glorifies the power of God.

'O VIRIDITAS DIGITI DEI'
The Green Voice of
Hildegard of Bingen

ALICE SPAWLS

Transcript of a lecture by Dr A. Spawls delivered in the year C-19 (corona year zero) at the first Speculative Mysticism conference. The venue is virtual: attendees are encouraged to watch footage of the forest at Disibodenberg and to listen, at reduced volume, to the accompanying playlist. At the start, the following words flash up on the screen: Where the rivers come together, build a church. Tributaries of the Rhine: Glan und Nahe, Neckar und Main.

Thank you all for travelling so far – virtually if not literally – to dwell for a short time with Hildegard of Bingen. Hildegard's is a voice piercing the darkness, speaking to us in an unknown language, creating an

unheard music. There is much that remains unknow-
able to us about her life and authorship, beginning
with the details of her birth. Her own account gives the
date 1100 years since the birth of Christ, or 920 years
pre–C-19 in the new calendar. It is more likely that she
was born two years earlier, in Bermersheim, not far
from the great bishoprics of Mainz, Speyer and Worms.
She grew up to the sound of trees and rivers, bees, bells
and horses drawing carts of salt along the Hellweg,
the Alte Salzstrasse, which carried valuable salt across
Europe. There was singing: not as simple diversion,
but as formal religious expression. She was a tenth
child, promised at birth as a tithe, a gift to the church.
As a young girl she was given into the care of Jutta of
Sponheim, a noblewoman who had taken solemn vows
at the age of twenty, withdrawing to a life of solitude
and spirituality. Hildegard became her companion.
On All Saints' Day in 1112 they were enclosed at the
Benedictine monastery at Disibodenberg.

Sequestration was a birth and a death. The *Rek-
lusin* went shrouded and barefooted to her new home.
She lay on leaves on the stone-cold floor. The bishop
blessed her with holy water. Two candles were lit and
she placed them on the altar. The congregation said
prayers and celebrated Mass. The funeral antiphon
was sung. The rites of the dying were read. She

entered her *gloriosum hunc carcarem*, her glorious prison, singing the antiphon for Psalm 131:14. 'This is my rest for ever: here will I dwell; for I have desired it.' She entered not in death but in abundance. She entered not silent but singing.

The monastery at Disibodenberg now lies in ruins, surrounded by pine trees, but it was fresh and unfinished when Hildegard entered. The noises of building and construction must have continually interrupted the Divine Office, the prayers that gave the day its shape and harmony. Matins began shortly after midnight. At dawn, Lauds. At half past six, Prime; just after eight, Terce. At noon: Sext. Nones in the afternoon, then Vespers, and at dusk, Complines. At Disibodenberg Hildegard was instructed in the singing of antiphons, or Psalms, a little Latin and such theological education as was required. It is said that she learned to play the ten-stringed psaltery, and perhaps she did. It seems she taught herself a great deal, fortified by everything she came across, strengthening a will and a voice that was, at least for the time being, sequestered away.

The nuns at Disibodenberg were an adjunct to the monks, fewer in number and dependent on their male counterparts for religious guidance, for Mass and Communion, for writing and books. Jutta taught Hildegard while also observing her, recognising, according to the *Vita domnae Juttae inclusae*, an unusual vitality in her young charge. Where Jutta practised mortification of the flesh and fasting, Hildegard was subjected to involuntary ailments. Illnesses of both mind and body repeatedly felled her, and it was only years later that she described the visions that accompanied these ailments – visions of religious and cosmic scenes.

After Jutta's death in 1136, Hildegard became an abbess, in charge of the other nuns, whose number had grown (or rather, she became *magistra*, because the women's community at Disibodenberg did not hold official status). She wrote for the first time of her experiences in a letter to Bernard, Abbott of Clairvaux:

Father, I am greatly disturbed by a vision which has appeared to me through divine revelation, a vision seen not with my fleshly eyes but only in my spirit. Wretched, and indeed more than wretched in my womanly condition, I have from earliest childhood seen great marvels which my tongue has no power to express, but which the Spirit of God has taught me that I may believe. Steadfast gentle father, in your kindness respond to me, your unworthy servant, who has never, from her earliest childhood, lived one hour free from anxiety . . . Through this vision which touches my heart and soul like a burning flame, teaching me profundities of meaning, I have an inward understanding of the Psalter, the Gospels, and other volumes. Nevertheless,

I do not receive this knowledge in German. Indeed, I have no formal training at all, for I know how to read only on the most elementary level, certainly with no deep analysis. But please give me your opinion in this matter, because I am untaught and untrained in exterior material, but am only taught inwardly, in my spirit. Hence my halting, unsure speech.

Hildegard's speech was halting and unsure because of the possible implications of her visions, but also because of her incomplete education in Latin. It may have been around this time that she began to design her *lingua ignota*, her unknown language. Bernard didn't discourage her, and with the help of the monk Volmar, who became her loyal secretary, she began to record the 'soul visions', as she described them. The first volume, *Scivias*, is divided into three sections (an echo of the Trinity) and deals with the Creation and the Fall, the coming of Christ, the Church and the kingdom yet to come. She also began to compose songs, fourteen of which were included in *Scivias*, pairs of antiphons and responsories that came to her directly in her visions.

It was Hildegard's duty as abbess to lead the chants and choose the liturgy, but her compositions are far more than that. The sequence in *Scivias* opens with an antiphon for Mary, '*O splendidissima gemma*', which celebrates the Virgin through a series of bright images:

a jewel infused with light, a flowering branch, the sun itself. The notes modulate up and over the octave, the melismas longest and highest on the words *serenum*, *creavit* and *voluit* ('serene', 'created' and 'willed'). Hildegard returned again and again to such imagery: sweet perfumes, greenness, honeycombs, spring water, gold, flashing gems. It is remarkable that the greatest body of music attributed to any one person in this period should come from a young abbess with little formal training or education, and for music to be only one of her many spheres of invention. In comparison with other religious compositions of the period, hers are characterised by their expressiveness and freedom, their ornamentation and upward leaps. Perhaps their irregularity owes something to the secular love songs of the *Minnesänger* (German minstrels) or perhaps it was the relative isolation of Disibodenberg and Hildegard's autonomy that allowed her to produce works of such exuberence. This is how she accounted for her sonic creativity: 'Then I saw the lucent sky, in which I heard different kinds of music, marvellously embodying all the meanings I had heard before.'

The feelings of the monks of Disibodenberg on discovering the visions and creations of their abbess can only be imagined. A delegation took a copy of

Scivias to the Synod of Trier in 1147, where parts were read aloud to the Pope. The synod considered cases of heresy and excommunication, and Hildegard could have been silenced, but Bernard of Clairvaux spoke on her behalf and she was granted papal approval to continue recording everything she saw in her visions. This made her the first woman to be given express permission to write theological treatise, and with it the approval to speak openly of her visions. Women were forbidden to preach but in effect that is what Hildegard did. Her fame began to grow, along with her correspondence. Her many surviving letters show that she was firm with the highest and meek with the lowest. She gave short shrift to her critics, though her authority – vindicated by her visions – is tempered by the appropriate caveats (her feebleness, femininity, the divine injunction).

Around 1148 Hildegard received a vision telling her to set out to a new place, at the meeting of two rivers, and to form her own monastery there. She asked her abbot for his permission, and when he denied she sought the approval of the Archbishop of Mainz, who granted it. She fell ill, becoming temporarily paralysed, until the abbot relented. The monks of Disibodenberg were reluctant to lose the source of their fame and wealth, and Hildegard still needed their support and protection, spiritual as well as practical. A dance began: entreat, avoid, persuade, then charge ahead. Hildegard didn't like to wait. She moved her nuns to the side of a steep hill, the Rupertsberg, overlooking the River Nahe where it meets the Rhine. There was almost nothing there – a few farm buildings and a chapel – and her nuns, accustomed to the comforts of Disibodenberg, struggled with the poverty of their conditions while Hildegard oversaw the construction of their new home. Slowly, a fine site came into being, and Hildegard began to receive gifts that would secure their future: a mill, the dowries of several new initiates, houses, vineyards, tithes and servants.

It was at Rupertsberg, with the assistance of Volmar and her beloved nun, Richardis, that the beautiful illustrated manuscript of *Scivias* was produced, and the second and third volumes of her visionary theology recorded. Her songs were collected into a cycle, the *Symphonia armoniae celestium revelationum*, and her morality play, *Ordo Virtutum* ('Play of the Virtues'), was recorded and performed. The *Ordo Virtutum* dramatised Hildegard's theology as described in *Scivias*, celebrating women's virtue as the means of man's salvation. The human souls and sixteen female virtues sing in plainchant, while the role of the Devil (perhaps played by Volmar) is spoken, with no musical setting. Hildegard wished her nuns to appear like the women in her visions, like Saint Ursula, one of her favourite subjects, who gathered around her a flock of virgins, 'a garden of apples and the flowers of all flowers'. Against all religious custom and protocol, Hildegard and her nuns, who were drawn entirely from the nobility, wore white silk and gold diadems, their hair long and loose. The practice was criticised, but her critics had to weigh their words. Hildegard brooked no dissent: it was, she said, married women and the lower classes who made such garments alluring or defiled them with vanity. For holy virgins, the white vestment signified their prelapsarian innocence and dedication to Christ; the crown their submission to the Trinity.

Hildegard, with her agile reasoning and forceful argument, had her way in many matters. Her cosmology brought woman, through the Virgin Mary, to the centre of religious life. She was the sun and God the eagle; she was the font, the flower, the material of holiness – what we might now call the *Powerfrau*. She was 'unwomanly' in nearly every respect, yet she used her womanhood as shield and sword, to deflect and parry blows. Her theology was conservative and rigorous, but idiosyncratic, aesthetically rich. It is through the two great crises of her life that we see her under creative and spiritual duress. The first was the removal of Richardis to Bassum, where she had been offered the post of abbess. Hildegard undertook everything in her power to prevent the departure, writing to Richardis's family, the archbishop and the Pope claiming that she was unprepared for the office and that those who supported her were motivated by arrogance. When these appeals failed, she wrote to Richardis herself, a letter of piety and pain: 'Why have you forsaken me like an orphan? Let all who have grief like mine mourn with me, all who, in the love of God, have had such great love in their hearts and minds for a person as I have had for you.' Is Richardis the model for the souls in the *Ordo Virtutum* who lose their way, or for her vision of Ursula, 'a dripping honeycomb . . . who yearned to embrace the Lamb of God, honey and milk beneath her tongue'? Or is it foolish to ask such a simple question and more fruitful to observe with wonder the force of spirit that could argue with popes, hear music in the spheres and write in self-fashioned languages.

The second crisis came at the very end of Hildegard's life, when Rupertsberg was wealthy and flourishing. One of its privileges was the burial of local nobles, and a scandal occurred when the clergy of Mainz demanded the disinterment of a nobleman who had supposedly been excommunicated. Hildegard refused, citing a vision, and in response the nuns were forbidden from singing the Divine Office or celebrating Mass. Hildegard knew she was approaching death and the loss of the sacrament was a heavy spiritual burden. The disappearance of song and music from the everyday life of the monastery must have been a catastrophe. In her letters of appeal, she expressed her philosophy of music:

> In order to recall that divine, sweet melody of praise which Adam, in company with the angels, enjoyed in God before his fall . . . for this reason the holy prophets, inspired by [the Spirit they had received], were called for this purpose: not only to compose psalms and canticles (by which the hearts of listeners would be inflamed) but also to construct various kinds of musical instruments to enhance these songs of praise with melodic strains.
>
> Thereby, both through the form and quality of the instruments, as well as through the meaning of the words which accompany them, those who hear might be taught, as we said above, about inward things, since they have been admonished and aroused by outward things.
>
> Men of zeal and wisdom have imitated the holy prophets and have themselves, with human skill, invented several kinds of musical instruments, so that they might be able to sing for the delight of their souls, and they accompanied their singing with instruments played with the flexing of the fingers, recalling, in this way, Adam, who was formed by God's finger, which is

the Holy Spirit. For, before he sinned, his voice had the sweetness of all musical harmony.

The interdict was lifted in March 1979, six months before her death, and her voice still reaches us, in the midst of darkness and ecological decay, through the virtual interface, beyond the virus.

NOTE

Quotes are drawn from Hildegard of Bingen's *Scivias* (translated by Columba Hart and Jane Bishop), and her letters collected in *The Personal Correspondence of Hildegard of Bingen* (translated and edited by Joseph L. Baird). The lyric 'a garden of apples and the flowers of all flowers' is from her 'Responsory to St Ursula and the Eleven Thousand Virgins' (translated by Lawrence Rosenwald).

The polymath **Hildegard of Bingen** (1098-17 September 1179) was a mystic, scientist, composer, herbalist and inventor of one of the earliest known constructed languages by a woman. Born in the Rhineland, Hildegard was educated from the age of eight at the Benedictine monastery at Mount St Disibode, later becoming an Abbess. She experienced prophetic visions since childhood and spent many years writing the visionary works *Scivias, Liber Vitae Meritorum* and *Liber Divinorum Operum*. Unusually for her time, she travelled and preached throughout southern Germany, Switzerland and as far as Paris. She died on 17 September 1179. She was formally canonized in 2012 by Pope Benedict XVI.

Huw Lemmey is a novelist, artist and critic living in Barcelona. He is the author of three novels: *Unknown Language, Red Tory: My Corbyn Chemsex Hell* (Montez Press, 2019), and *Chubz: The Demonization of my Working Arse* (Montez Press, 2016). He writes on culture, sexuality and cities for the *Guardian, Frieze, Flash Art, Tribune, TANK, The Architectural Review, Art Monthly, New Humanist, Rhizome, The White Review,* and *L'Uomo Vogue,* amongst others. He writes the weekly essay series *utopian drivel* and is the co-host of *Bad Gays.*

Bhanu Kapil is a British-Indian artist and poet. She is the author of five full length works of poetry/prose, including *How to Wash a Heart* (2020), *Ban en Banlieue* (2015) and *Schizophrene* (2012). She is a winner of the Windham-Campbell Prize 2020 and is currently the Judith E. Wilson Poetry Fellow at the University of Cambridge.

Alice Spawls is a writer and editor at the *London Review of Books*. She is a co-founder of Silver Press, the feminist publisher.